Carly Remembers

Carly Remembers

is a fictional psychological thriller that weaves a story of a woman's journey through recovery from sexual abuse and incest. Inspired by real-life therapy.

R.S. Nichols

ISBN 979-8-9886076-0-1

Book Cover by R.S. Nichols

First Edition 2026

My Most Grateful Thanks

My most grateful thanks to William F. Hager, who brilliantly helped with a developmental edit, before I even understood this process, and suggested changes throughout this book, allowing my story to grow into the story it is today.

Additionally, I wish to thank the various people who helped me edit my book. One of the main editors was Stefanie Engstrom, who thoroughly and thoughtfully reviewed this and kindly provided feedback and suggestions to improve its message.

Dedicated to

All the abuse or incest survivors who have never had a voice; never give up,

and

to Quiseeker, my muse.

CHAPTER ONE

BROKEN AND BLOODIED

Harold glances up from his place perched atop a chipped metal stool in front of the small flat-screen television hanging from a broken metal bracket in the corner of the New Brunswick 7-Eleven. An old rerun of an entry from the *Death Wish* trilogy fights through poor reception, blurred with static.

Bored and drowsy, Harold glances at his watch: 10:17. *Oh man, 43 minutes to go.*

Bob, the night shift manager, who proudly displays a name tag reflecting his title on the front pocket of his white, short-sleeved, button-down work shirt, leans on the counter behind the register, the old wood groaning under his three hundred pounds. "Harold, why don't you go out and walk the lot for trash. It's about that time. I'll mop up."

"Okay." Harold sighs, straightening his legs, wincing at the pop in his knee and creak in his ankle. He yawns, stretches his arms toward the ceiling, hearing another pop in his neck that rattles down his spine. He runs his hands over his head, through hair thinning faster than it can replenish. At least the cool air will feel nice and help him get through the end of his shift.

He shuffles past the newspaper stand–*the lotto's only fifteen million today, not worth the effort*–and in front of the cash register, where he notices a harsh look from his manager.

The door chimes on his way out into the night. He begins his survey in the usual spot, at the far corner of the front parking lot, looking for trash, hoping to find some money dropped by some poor, unfortunate soul. *Maybe I'll find another $10 bill.*

Harold strolls around, scanning the ground. Near the dented green dumpster, resting against a brick facade, he notices a wrinkly unidentified bunch of papers and rushes over.

Bummer. Only a hot-dog boat smeared with mustard and a plastic Big Gulp with half-melted ice, swarming with ants. He pulls a black trash bag from the frayed back pocket of his blue Dickies. He picks up the refuse, wishing he'd remembered to wear his rubber cleaning gloves, and sticks it in the trash bag.

A light sprinkle of rain falls from the clouded night sky. Harold glances up, sees the faded lights of a plane on its descent into New Brunswick International, glowing through the low cloud cover, hears the rumble of its engines. He rounds the corner, strolls toward the back of the lot. He blinks a few times, gazing at something in a crumpled mass on the ground.

Is that a body?

He races over, dropping his trash bag, and scrapes his knee on the cracked asphalt crouching down to take a closer look.

A woman lies facedown, bruised, blood pooling under her head. She's dressed in a short black skirt, with a torn taupe-colored halter top, and barefoot. Gashes covering her bare arms and legs, pour forth their red liquid of life. One of her arms is twisted at a perilous angle. Harold winces just considering it.

He leans up, hyperventilating, for what seems like forever. He stands, uncertain what to do, then runs back into the store.

Harold runs in yelling in rapid fire spurts, "Bob, there's a dead girl out back! Oh my God, call someone! What do we do? Call the police? The doctor? Um, a funeral home? Quick, call 911, they'll know what to do."

"Jesus, breathe, man," Bob says, his face going paler than usual. He drops his mop and shuffles outside.

"She's over here," Harold shouts while pointing. He peeks around Bob as they approach the sprawled-out girl. Dumbfounded, Harold stares at the girl, then at Bob.

Bob stammers, "You-you're right, a de-dead girl!"

They run back inside the store. Bob grabs the cordless phone. He attempts to dial 911 but misdials, connecting on the second attempt. "We have a dead body here," he shouts. "Send someone over–the police or something–quick!" Bob hangs up.

They head back outside.

Almost immediately, the phone rings.

Harold grabs the phone. "Um…7…um…Eleven."

A lady on the other end states, "Sir, we just received a call from this number stating that there's a dead body at your location."

Harold responds, a quiver in his voice, "Yes, that was Bob, the night supervisor."

"Bob, your supervisor, is dead?"

"No! He called you all. Yes. We have a dead girl! Come quick!"

"This is the New Brunswick Emergency Response Services. Please give me your address."

"Um...5469...wait, no, 4569 Fourth Street. Please, send someone right away!"

Harold hangs up, glances back at his watch: 10:35. He sighs, exasperated. No way he'll be finished with his shift on time tonight.

CHAPTER TWO

THE CALL

Detective John Patrick Daugherty, a 30-year-old, special victims detective, sits in his gun metal gray Dodge Charger, engine running, heat blasting. He eats a mashed-bean-and-faux-pepperjack vegan burrito, wishing he'd gone for the chili-habanero sauce Xochitl's Café had offered, while staring out a window fogging up to near opacity. There's no snow tonight but it's damn cold–enough to feel it in your lungs. A new down comforter on his bed beckons from his apartment.

He hears a familiar voice crackle on his radio. The New Brunswick Police 911 dispatch operator spreads the call. "We have a possible 187, behind the 7-Eleven on Fourth Street. Any homicide detective, please respond."

Another voice interjects. Captain Monahan tells dispatch, "Jim Franklin's homicide on duty. Send him."

An unknown voice queries, "Does this look like it could be another of The Tailor's victims?"

"Unconfirmed," says Monahan, "but if it is, we need to be on-site, right away."

Daugherty's pulse quickens. *The Tailor*. An investigation that brings excitement at the prospect of making a breakthrough in a very public, high-profile, career-making case. At the same time, he is all too aware of the gruesome nature of this killer's methods and his pervasive and slippery ability to elude capture that could send Daugherty down a rabbit hole of frustration leading to a futile chase.

Daugherty hesitates to speak up, knowing how close he is to the scene of tonight's incident.

Another voice breaks through on the radio. "Get paramedics down here, stat. The vic is still alive."

The captain yells, "Hey, Daugherty, we have a 245 vic down at the 7-Eleven on Fourth Street. It's yours now. CS is on-site."

"Thought we had a 187?" Daugherty says, quelling the pit in his stomach.

"Waitin' on you now."

Daugherty runs his fingers over the newly minted silver shield he earned less than a year ago, and revs his engine.

***

Down the block, two rights and a left bring him to the 7-Eleven. He ducks beneath the yellow tape encircling the area behind the store. Before being asked, he pulls out his badge and displays it to the log-duty officer, dressed in a crisp, pressed, dark-blue uniform. "Daugherty. Victims. Who's in charge on-site?"

The log duty officer, points to the man in the blue shirt. "Lead CSU guy is Maxwell Easton. He and the boys from the lab are over there waiting on you, sir."

"Thanks."

Daugherty glances over and sees a tall man, pushing fifty, with a receding widow's peak, his hands stuffed deep into the pockets of a dime-store trench coat.

"Jim Franklin. Hey, man," Daugherty says, reaching out to shake his friend's hand. "Captain sent the call to me. The vic wasn't dead?"

"That's right," Jim says. "Saw her move and requested paramedics, then asked for someone from Victims. I've got another case, suspected serial killer, thinking maybe she's one that got away."

Daugherty glances up. "Yeah?" An uneasy feeling rises in his mind.

"When you get back to the house, come see me, we'll talk."

"M'kay, man."

Daugherty walks over to the lead CS guy, who is squatting down to the cracked asphalt. "Easton?"

Easton waves his latex-gloved hand in greeting. "You Daugherty?"

"Yep." Daugherty nods. "So, what's the story?"

"Well, we initially thought we had a 187. Detective Franklin realized the victim wasn't dead and called it in. We stood down until she was bundled off to the hospital and waited for you. The paramedics left right before you got here."

"We ready to do this, then?" Daugherty asks as he slips on his green latex gloves.

"Yeah, let's go."

Easton motions to the forensics team to follow. He likewise beckons to the log-duty officer. "Who was the first to arrive at the scene, and who set up the initial perimeter?

"It was me. I was here first and taped off the area."

"Does everything appear like it did when you first got here? Aside from the victim?"

The log-duty officer looks around, glancing at his clipboard. "Yes, sir, it appears to be in the same condition as when I arrived at 10:47, apart from the vic, who was transported by paramedics at 10:53 to Good Sam."

The group attends to their own tasks. Daugherty strolls the area, rubbing his chin between his thumb and index fingers, his thick, sharp scruff a reminder that he neglected to shave that morning and the morning before. "Who found the victim?"

"A pair of clerks working the late shift. Harold Lincoln found the victim. I told him to stay inside the store. The other's Bob Gibson. He called it in. I asked him to wait outside, over there. No one else at the scene."

"Thank you."

After circling the entire lot like a flock of geese landing in a field, the group congregates where the girl was found. Daugherty observes the pool of blood at the top of the chalk outline, noting the purse laying near the outline of one hand. He beckons the forensics guy. "Hey, Williams, come here and get your pictures. I want to see what's in the purse."

Williams kneels and, after a few clicks from several different angles, rises. "Okay, I got the immediate scene."

Daugherty reaches down and picks up the purse. He places it in a big plastic bag, marking it: *7-Eleven victim-October 24, 1998.*

Squatting down, he places the bag on the asphalt. Holding open the purse, he rummages around, retrieving the victim's driver's license. He scribbles down her name. *Carly McCulley*. He adds her home address and driver's license number, then stands. "I have everything I need here. I'll leave you guys to your work."

He strides into the store through the double sliding glass doors and sees Harold Lincoln sitting behind the counter. He offers one hand and flashes his badge with the other. "Hello, I'm Detective Daugherty from the New Brunswick Police, Special Victims Investigator. Do you mind if I ask you some questions?" Daugherty gets out his pad and pen.

Harold shakes his head. "No, sir."

"First, what's your name?"

"Harold Lincoln."

"Tell me what happened, everything you remember. Take your time."

Harold trembles. "I was out walkin' the lot, um, picking up the trash, like I always do this time o'night. I came 'round the corner and found the girl out back. We thought she was dead."

"Go on."

"I ran and told Bob, and we called 911."

"Did you see anything suspicious?"

Harold stutters. "N-no, sir, it's been a slow night. After we called, we just waited until the police came.

After they came, one of them started puttin' yellow tape all 'round the back of the lot. One officer with the clipboard told me to wait inside."

"What time was this?"

"'Bout 10:45 or so."

"How long have you worked here?"

"'Bout three years."

"What's your job title?"

"Night clerk and porter."

"Have you ever seen the girl before?"

"Um," Harold mumbles, shaking his head. "Uh, no, sir."

"Thank you."

Detective Daugherty walks back outside and over to the other clerk. He offers his hand. "Detective Daugherty, New Brunswick Police, I'm a Special Victims Investigator. Do you mind if I ask you some questions?"

Bob shakes his head. "Not at all, sir."

"What's your name?"

"Bob Gibson."

"Did you see anything suspicious this evening?"

Bob shakes his head. "No. We didn't have many customers for the last few hours. It's been real quiet."

"What time was this?"

"I don't know, after 10:25 maybe. I'm not sure."

"How long have you worked here?"

"Since 1991, little over seven years now."

"What's your position here?"

"Night manager. Hoping to get onto days, eventually."

"Have you ever seen the girl before?"

"Not that I recall."

"Okay, tell me what happened. Tell me everything you remember. Please, take your time."

Head down, Bob responds, "I was mopping when Harold came running in like a crazy man, shouting there was a dead girl outside. We ran out and saw her lying there." Bob points over to where she had been lying. "Then I came back in and called 911. Then we went outside and waited for the police. They got here real fast with their sirens on and everything and started to tape off the area with that yellow 'keep out' tape. I seen that on the cop shows before. Then, one of the officers told Harold to get back inside the store, and he told me to go over and wait by the police car. I seen the one cop check the body and then get on his radio and say she wasn't dead. They outlined her body in chalk. One of the other cops was taking pictures, and then the ambulance came and took her away, then you arrived."

"Thank you."

Daugherty glances toward Easton, still surveying the scene. "I'm done here. Let me know if you guys find anything interesting."

"Sure thing, Detective, we'll let you know."

Detective Daugherty passes a uniformed officer. "Where did paramedics take our vic?"

"Good Sam."

"I'm going to head over to the hospital now, if anyone asks."

Daugherty slides into the seat of his Charger and closes the door. He puts his hands on the steering wheel, gaze fixed on the scene. *How did you end up in that parking lot?*

He glances down at his worn black leather messenger bag on the passenger-side floor, stuffed full of papers, then back at the banker's box ready to fall apart and spill its bulging contents all over his back seat. Time for the hunt to begin. He sighs.

Nothing like a good mystery to start off the weekend.

--

Daugherty strides into Good Samaritan Hospital's emergency room through two thick sliding glass doors framed in stainless steel. The sharp, unmistakable hospital odor, a combination of bleach and Pine-Sol, lingers in his nostrils. He blinks away the artificial glow from the fluorescent lights lining the ceiling. Crackling pages emanate from speakers set high on the walls.

All he needs is one bit of information to kick off his investigation.

He approaches the desk, manned by the nurse on duty, her bifocals hanging low on the angled bridge of her nose. "A girl was just brought in," he says. "A Ms. Carly McCulley. I need to ask her some questions."

The nurse doesn't look up. "Family?"

"No, ma'am, Special Victims Investigator from New Brunswick PD."

The nurse glances at her screen, clacks a few keys. "Doctors are working on her in emergency right now. From the notes, it shows she's unconscious but stable."

"Any information you can give me?"

"Sorry, Officer, got nothing else for you."

Daugherty sighs. "Okay, well, here's my card. When she wakes up, please give me a call?"

The nurse nods. "Will do."

As Daugherty strolls back through the glass doors, he realizes he is spinning his wheels at a time he can little afford to. He sits down behind the wheel of his Charger, sighing and rubbing his temples.

No forward progress, only stasis. Like a wall standing in his path halting his movement. The stacks of files remain right where they were when he'd pulled into the parking lot, right where they were this morning and the day before.

He guns the engine, tires screeching as he leaves the hospital, questions plaguing his thoughts, trying to scrape through the consuming frustration.

Who are you, Ms. McCulley?

CHAPTER THREE

BACK AT THE HOUSE

Detective Daugherty enters the precinct's central crime-task office area, his worn leather messenger bag slung over his shoulder. Numerous desks populate the large open area, scattered around the inner section facing each other in groups of four. A monitor sits atop each desk, alongside piles of documents and folders, overflowing outboxes filled to the brim, and inboxes stuffed with files holding endless to-do lists.

Detective Daugherty heads for Jim Franklin's "office," a desk partitioned from the rest of the room by six-foot-tall cloth-covered dividers.

Daugherty peeks around the corner and sees Jim, his dark-brown hair graying at the temples, weather-worn skin an unwelcome reward from years of walking the beat. He's hunched over a thick, light-brown file laden with papers and photos.

Jim looks up, rocks back in his creaking swivel chair, and smiles, then his face changes to something more somber. "Hey."

"Hey, man. Last night you asked me to come see you. What's up? Does this have anything to do with my 245 investigation?"

"Yeah. Have you had a chance to question her yet?"

"No. She was unconscious last time I checked. I told 'em to call when she wakes."

Jim furrows his brow, his jaw set hard. "You know the big case I've been working on?"

"Yeah, I've heard of it."

"Well, the marks on our new vic's wrists, the cuts on her legs, seem very similar to the MO of the killer we've been tracking. No real hard science behind this yet, just my gut tellin' me it's possible."

"The Tailor?" A wave of adrenaline shoots through Daugherty's body as he considers this.

"Follow me."

Daugherty follows Jim down the hall into a conference room. "Inviting me into the homicide sanctuary? I feel honored," Daugherty says, half joking. Photographs of victims blanket various bulletin boards sitting on tables covering half of the room. A whiteboard stands at one end of the room with a comprehensive list of commonalities between each of the murder victims' injuries, how they died, where they were found, and other pertinent circumstances surrounding their deaths.

The amount of clutter blanketing the small room almost suffocates Daugherty, a claustrophobic reaction reminding him of his own stack of files weighing him down.

"See this?" Jim says, pointing to pictures of various victims' wrists and legs. "These marks and wounds look like the ones I noticed on your vic yesterday. I haven't had a chance to see the forensics photos from the scene, but I'd bet my Packers tickets they're a match."

Daugherty circles the room taking in all the details of the photographs on the walls. "Mouths sewn shut?"

Jim nods. "Yep."

"What can you tell me? Are there any leads? What do these victims have in common? Is it how they died? Are these all of the victims? How long has this case been open?"

"Whoa, man, so many questions. Well, first of all, there are the binding marks left on the victims' wrists. See here." He points to close-up pictures depicting deep welts of blunted purples, yellows, and greens encircling the victims' wrists. "These men and women were all handcuffed, beaten, cut, and tortured to varying degrees. Each had their eyes gouged out and mouths sewn shut, plus their right hands severed. The men had their penises cut off and stuffed inside their mouths before they were sewn shut."

Detective Daugherty grimaces.

"This appears to have all been done while the victims were still alive."

"Still alive? Wow, really?"

"So far, we have five likely victims–three men, two women–not including your live one yesterday."

"Mine?" Shaking his head. "Was sex involved somehow?"

"Well, maybe. There's some really sick, messed-up shit involved here. There's evidence of *some* type of sexual activity in most of the victims, but the culprit must have worn a condom, because we found no DNA evidence that links to anyone in our databases. As to leads, well, that's what I'm working on, but no, nothing solid. They all seemed to have died from massive blood loss. I've been working on this for the past few weeks."

"Are you working up a profile? Motive?"

"That's always the question. My guess is, this is a guy who's very..."

"Sick?"

"I was gonna say *angry*."

"Ya think? There's probably more going on than just anger."

"I think it's too early to be seriously making statements, but I'm thinking we're looking at a male, late 40s or early 50s. Control freak, working a menial-type job, probably abused as a kid, who feels powerless and gets off on some level from meting out a ritualistic type of...I don't know, some sort of a twisted form of justice on his victims."

"Ritualistic justice? Really?" Daugherty swallows hard, down a dry throat.

"Well, the severed right hand, the gouged-out eyes, that probably means something to the killer. The sewn-up mouths and eyes probably also holds some symbolism. I could guess, but it would be just a guess. I think your vic got away before this killer was able to finish his work."

"How do you know it's a guy?"

"Well, in my experience, female killers are a different breed. They usually kill for financial gain and aren't usually *as* brutal."

"Really? Gives me something to think about while I'm investigating."

"I'll be very interested to find out what your 245 vic has to say. What did you say her name was again?"

"Carly McCulley."

"Let me know once she wakes. I want to question her as soon as possible. In the meantime, I want you to keep low-profile surveillance on her at all times. I don't want to alarm her unless this escalates somehow."

"Okay. I have a guy stationed by her room at the hospital now. I'll make sure we keep an eye on her.

I've checked both her places of work, talked with her bosses and co-workers, neighbors, and family. No leads."

"Both places of work?" Jim queries.

"Yeah. She has two part-time jobs. One transcribing probation reports and the other typing reports for a private investigator.

"While I was checking out Ms. McCulley's apartment this morning, I came across a message on her answering machine from one of her friends. Can you run a search on him? I asked Tina, but she said she's backlogged. This seems a little more urgent now in light of what you just told me."

"Okay, but you owe me, again. What's the name?"

After consulting his note pad, Daugherty states, "Robert Hoy. Not sure of the spelling."

Jim clacks a string of keys, keeping Daugherty on edge.

"M'kay. Let me know what you find. Talk to you later," Daugherty says, heading back to his desk.

Jim nods.

Daugherty's head spins with Jim's revelation. That Carly could have escaped a serial killer added a whole new dimension to the case, one that moved it from the bottom of Daugherty's stack to closer to the top.

***

As Daugherty pecks out his report on the keyboard, the phone rings. Franklin asks, "Hey, can you come over to my desk for a minute? I have the information you asked me to look up on your 245 vic's friend."

Daugherty approaches Jim's cubicle with guarded anticipation.

"I got the info on Robert Hoy you asked for." Jim hands him a manila folder. "Here's what I've found."

"So, tell me about what you dug up."

"There's the file. Read it."

"The CliffsNotes version," Daugherty prods.

"He's divorced with a daughter who doesn't live with him. He's an artist who lives in a loft in the Heights, an artsy location. He works for CBS as a storyboard motion-graphic artist and has been for the last six years, working on sports and football game graphics, among other things. The best I could tell, he's been involved with Ms. McCulley for the past couple years. He pays his taxes, his child support, and pretty much keeps his nose clean." Jim arches his eyebrows. "He does run in the BDSM circles."

"BDSM? Really?" Daugherty shakes his head, opening the manila folder, glancing at its contents. "I don't get it."

"What don't you get?"

"Hurting someone or tying someone up and having sex. Why do that?"

"You're such a Boy Scout! It's so much more complex than that. Come on, be honest, doesn't it turn you on, on some level? Having total power over someone you can control completely?"

Daugherty considers this and pushes back. "Sex is supposed to be with someone you love, not someone you want to hurt."

"You need to get out more. It's not about hurting someone. It's really a lot more complex than what you are thinking. At its core, it's about power and control. There's a power exchange that occurs that's very intoxicating. There's lots of kinky stuff out there at one end of the continuum that is just a little weird, to some extreme weirdness, at the other end of the continuum--real shocking shit."

Shaking his head, Daugherty queries, "Our boy here into the extreme weird stuff?"

"Our boy here, not too weird."

"Well, thanks for the info. This kinda puts this investigation into an entirely new realm."

"Anytime. Remember you owe me."

As Daugherty heads back to his desk, he glances over his shoulder and asks, "Hey, how do you know so much about BDSM?"

Shaking his head, smirking and waging his index finger, Franklin says, “Taking the Fifth on that one, man.”

Daugherty shakes his head. He’s known Detective Franklin for a decade, but can’t help but wonder if he truly knows him–if he truly knows anyone, for that matter.

CHAPTER FOUR

WAKING UP

(Two weeks later)

"Hello, this is Detective Daugherty."

"Hi, Detective, this is Rose from Good Sam. We had your name on file for patient Carly McCulley."

"Yes."

"Well, she's awake now."

Daugherty smiles. "I'll be right over."

***

Where am I?

Carly opens her eyes. She glances around, struggles to sit up. Raising her left arm, she stares in disbelief at the cast extending from her knuckles to her elbow. Tape secures her fingers with a metal clip-on device pinched over the top of her index finger. The mass of tubes and wires on her right prevents her from raising that hand easily, but as she touches her nose, feels plastic tubing wrapped around her face and under her nose.

Panic sets in. She struggles with the tubing, trying to pull it back over her head.

A red-haired, middle-aged nurse with a kindly, weathered face enters her room, rushes to her side.

"Whoa, whoa, whoa," the nurse says. "Finally! You're awake, dear. How do you feel?"

Through a throat ragged and raw, Carly squeaks, clearing her throat. "Where am I?"

"You're at New Brunswick Good Samaritan Hospital. You've been here a couple weeks. I have some questions. Do you think you'd be up for that?"

Carly nods with hesitation.

"Do you know what year it is?"

"1998."

"Do you know what your name is?"

Pausing and thinking, Carly shakes her head. "I…I don't know."

"Do you know who the president is?"

The nurse moves around checking the tubes and readings on the machines as well as Carly's blood pressure and temperature, smiling the entire time.

Is she joking? I don't remember my name. "Bill Clinton, I think."

"Two out of three, not bad! Your stats look good. You took quite a blow to your head. How do you feel?"

Foggy, confused and exhausted, Carly responds, "Like…how did I get here?"

"An ambulance brought you in unconscious," the nurse says in a kindly sounding tone.

"I feel, um, I'm tired."

"I don't doubt it. You are okay, hun."

"My throat is really sore. Could I have some water?"

"Sure. Here you go." The nurse holds the drinking cup with a straw up to Carly's lips, then moves the rolling bedside stand closer.

"Thank you." The cooling water comforts Carly's throat.

"Just rest. If you need anything, just press this button. I'll be back to check in on you later."

Carly stares at the ceiling, the plasterboard tiles collected in groups of four. She wrinkles her nose at the sterile, chemical smell of the hospital, watches nurses, doctors, patients, and staff hustle by. Confused, she nervously glances around her spartan room, but sees no personal effects. Her room, like her mind–empty.

***

Detective Daugherty enters the hospital. *With any luck, Carly might still be awake and willing to answer a few questions.* He'd been nervous this case would stall with her medical condition prohibiting any progress.

As Daugherty gets off the elevator he glances at the sign–*Rooms 400 - 440*–with an arrow pointing to the right. He looks down the hall. Outside room 423 he sees an older officer, gray streaks highlighting his dark hair, sitting reading a book. Detective Daugherty walks up, extending his hand in greeting to the officer in the freshly pressed blues.

Looking up, the officer stands in formal greeting, "Detective Daugherty."

"Hello," looking down at the name above his badge, "Officer Clancey, right? I'm Detective Daugherty from downtown. Special Victims Unit. We spoke on the phone. I'm here to question Ms. McCulley. I understand she's awakened."

Officer Clancey stands and greets Detective Daugherty with a nod and smile. "Good morning. Yes, that's correct."

"Anyone come to visit her?" Daugherty brushes past him. "I'll only be a couple minutes."

"No one. Not while I've been on duty."

Detective Daugherty opens the large green door labeled *Room 423.* As he enters, he scans the drab, bluish-gray decor, sparsely furnished with a bed, a TV, a small-frame window on one side, a closet, and a door leading to the lavatory. A bouquet of fresh flowers sits on the table next to the bed. *What's that scent? Jasmine? Or is it lilacs? The TV's on?*

He looks to the bed, noticing Mr. McCulley appears to be asleep. Transfixed, Daugherty gazes at her and at the array of tubes and wires extending over her, connected to a silver monitor. *Good watchman, standing like an ever-vigilant sentry ready to sound the alarm in case anything is amiss.*

He jots down details of the girl's description in a small notebook pulled from his inner jacket pocket. Long, reddish-blond hair. Mid-twenties, about 5'5", maybe 125 pounds. Dark purple and green bruises conceal the middle of her face. *What kind of fucking animal did this?*

Though he's never met Carly, a sense of protectiveness sweeps over him. A dark sense of outrage rises inside him as her assault echoes the similarities with his sister's assault as he replays the gruesome details in his mind. *No difference between this guy and the one who raped Ann.*

Dejected, he turns to leave.

Clearing her throat first, Carly squeezes out a question, "Hello. Who are you?"

Daugherty glances back at Carly, who gazes up at him. Echoes of the dark magenta bruises shadow her eyes, giving them an eerie skull like quality. She pulls her bed covers higher.

Holding out his hand and speaking in his most cheerful voice, he says, "Hi, sorry, I'm Detective John Daugherty of the New Brunswick Police Department."

Carly smiles and attempts to offer her right hand but grimaces, extending her left hand instead.

"I didn't mean to wake you up. I've been anxious to talk to you." Detective Daugherty attempts to wave off the handshake, briefly touching Carly's fingers. "Oh, never mind the formality, my apologies." As his hand touches hers, he feels a surge of energy run through his body. He dismisses it and stays focused.

"How are you feeling?" Daugherty nervously asks.

"Sore. Tired." Carly attempts to scoot up higher into more of a sitting position in the bed, groaning as she does.

"To explain a bit about why I'm here; I collect victim's information, then help them deal with the trauma of whatever happened. For lack of a better description, I'm kind of a post-traumatic-event resource-support specialist and investigator."

Carly nods. "You think I'm a victim?"

"Yes, you are a victim of a crime that left you unconscious. I don't want to pressure you, but do you feel up to answering some questions?"

Carly, with her eyebrows furrowed, appearing confused or distressed, responds, "Well, I guess so."

"Do you know where you are?"

Smiling and bowing her head a bit, Carly says, "Um, the nurse told me."

"Do you know what happened to you? Do you have any idea how you ended up here, injured and unconscious?"

Carly groans, peering down at her hands and shaking her head. "The doctors and nurses asked me the same thing. I don't know what happened."

Even though Daugherty senses she might be growing weary, he presses a bit more. "Well, what's the last thing you do remember?"

Carly sighs. "The last thing I remember was leaving work, um…Tuesday night, I think. It's all kinda fuzzy."

"That was a couple weeks ago."

"What?" Carly responds with wide eyes and an open mouth. "A couple weeks ago? I'm having trouble focusing on…oh…I feel, um…woozy."

"You know, this can wait. You need to rest."

"No, no, I'm okay enough to talk a little more."

"Well, okay, but…."

"Where was I when...I don't remember...who, someone found me?"

"A night cashier at the 7-Eleven found you, over on Fourth Street. He didn't see how you got there. Apparently, you were around the side of the building away from the view of the cashiers."

Carly listens, eyes downcast. "Has anyone gone to my apartment? I think I might have pets. Do I have pets? Has anyone checked?"

Detective Daugherty responds, smiling. "I went over to your apartment to investigate right after they found you. I have been feeding your fish. You didn't have any other pets that I saw."

Carly nods. "Thank you."

"It's part of my job. To protect and to serve. Says so right on the badge." He smiles, doffing an imaginary hat. "Do you have any family you might want me to contact, if the hospital hasn't already done so? Do you remember anyone?"

"One of the nurses told me they called my cousin, I think, who lives in another state. She told them my parents are gone, and I don't think I have any siblings or other relatives close by."

Another nurse bursts into the room. "Carly needs her rest, Detective. Are you almost finished?"

"Yes, ma'am," Daugherty states obediently.

After checking Carly's tubes and monitoring equipment, the nurse leaves, an eyebrow arched in suspicion at Daugherty's promise.

"I understand that since you're awake now, they're going to let you go home. Since you don't have any family around, I'd be more than happy to drive you."

Carly nods.

Smiling, Detective Daugherty says, "Well I better get going. Don't want to incur that nurse's wrath. I'm glad you're awake. I'll be back tomorrow."

He exits into the hallway, leaving the door to close behind him with a soft click. He stops for a crash cart flying past, pushed by a frantic orderly.

"Keep a close eye on the girl," Daugherty says to Officer Clancy, before stepping onto the elevator. "I'll be back tomorrow to collect her." As it whirs downward, Daugherty takes in the worn numbers on the buttons, the graffiti scrawled into the metal button plate–elements most people usually take for granted or ignore. He hopes Carly can provide some details of what happened, or the odds of solving this case will sink faster than the elevator.

CHAPTER FIVE

BACK HOME

Detective Daugherty pulls his Charger up to the curb at the Good Samaritan Hospital's main entrance. He bounds out of the car, leaving the engine purring.

The automatic doors slide open, and a nurse pushes Carly outside in a wheelchair. She winces in the sunlight.

"Good morning," Daugherty says. "How's our patient?"

The nurse responds, "Eager to get out of here, I think."

Carly grimaces. "Everything hurts, but I'll live."

Daugherty and the nurse help Carly into the passenger seat, trying not to bump any still-healing areas on her body.

"Do you need some help with the seatbelt?" he asks.

"Um, I guess. Do I have to wear one? I think this will hurt my ribs."

"Well, yes, it's the law. Let's see, if we keep it slightly loose...."

Carly lets out a deep breath.

Daugherty nods to the nurse. "Thank you."

“Remind her she has to check back in with us in a week.”

“Will do, ma’am.”

Daugherty circles around the front of his car. He glances up to see Carly staring at him the whole way. He opens the door, clicks his seatbelt, and eases the car away from the hospital.

“How are you feeling? Have you had any memories return? Anything at all?”

“No, not really. I’ve been sleeping a lot. They gave me meds that make me feel fuzzy. All I want is…I dunno. I’ve been having weird dreams, but that’s not answering your question.”

A few turns and stoplights lead them to Carly’s building.

“Here we are.”

Daugherty steps out of the car and quickly moves around to the passenger side. He lets Carly lean on him as she gets out, going slowly, accentuating each movement.

“Does anything around here seem familiar? This building?”

Carly gazes around the neighborhood with a blank stare. “No, not really.”

Daugherty notices a man sitting in a dark-colored car down the block. The man watches, not moving. Daugherty makes a mental note but decides not to mention this, deciding to deal with one thing at a time. He’ll check in on their observer after he has Carly settled.

They make their way up the four chipped concrete steps, through a glass entry door that grates against its frame, and across the lobby's stained, frayed carpeting.

Once in the elevator, attempting to break the now awkward silence, Daugherty asks, "How are you doing? I'm concerned all the commotion leaving the hospital may have worn you out."

Carly shakes her head. "I'm tired and sore. I'm okay, I guess. Glad to be home."

The elevator doors open onto the hallway. Daugherty sticks his head out apparently scoping for bad guys. He helps Carly open the door to her apartment. As she steps in, he cheerfully states, "You're home!"

Carly looks around, observing piles of books and notepads laying all over the living room. A computer sits at one end of the dining-room table with a printer nearby.

"Do you remember anything?" Daugherty queries.

Frowning, Carly flatly states, "No." She sniffs the stale air. "That smell, the flowers, magnolia–that reminds me of something. Not sure what, but it reminds me of something."

Carly ambles around the living room, looking at everything, touching the pillows on the couch, peering at her fish. She reflexively puts some food in the tank. Shaking her head, "I don't remember."

"You need some groceries. When I was here before, I cleaned out the fridge because there were alien life-forms growing in there. Give me a list, and I'll run to the store for you."

Carly smiles. "That would be very nice of you." She walks over to her desk and writes down a list of groceries. "I don't have...I haven't gotten to...um...to the bank, but I'll pay you back as soon as I can. Can you go to the drugstore and get this prescription filled as well? The nurse said it's for pain. I don't know that I'll need it, but I want to have it just in case."

"Absolutely! Remember, to protect and to serve!" He takes the list and prescription from her and turns to leave. He hands Carly a business card. "Here's my number, if you need me while I'm gone. I'll be back in a flash."

Carly smiles. "Do detectives always play concierge?"

Daugherty laughs. "No, usually not, but this case is a bit of an exception."

"Thank you, Detective, for everything."

"Please, call me John. There's no need to be so formal."

"Okay, Detective--John," Carly says with a slight smile. "Thank you."

Daugherty skips down the concrete stairs in front of Carly's building to the sidewalk, glancing up and down the street. No sign of the car he had noticed on their way in or its apparently focused driver. He shoots a glance up the street, then back to his Charger.

***

After Detective Daugherty departs, Carly walks into her bedroom. A fluffy, white comforter lies crumpled in a pile on one side of the bed. Several books are stacked haphazardly on the adjoining nightstand. Three bookcases line the far wall holding hundreds of books, dozens of pictures, Rodin and Degas statues, and assorted handmade pottery, as well as a CD player and hundreds of CDs. Carly blankly glances at some of the books. Classical literature, science fiction, art-instruction guides, psychology and self-help books.

In the vacant spaces between the books and CDs are numerous framed photos laying face down on the shelves. She flips up a couple of the pictures and gazes at a photograph of a man, a woman, and a little girl, posed in a happy, family-style portrait. After glancing at the now-strange surroundings, trying to find some connection, she shudders, failing to recognize anything.

She steps into the bathroom and looks at herself in the mirror and gasps.

Astonished at her appearance, Carly slips her blouse over her head, drawing a twinge of pain. The remnants of a massive bruise, a pale mixture of yellow ocher, putrid green, and magenta, blots her pale skin around the faint echoes of stitches under her rib cage. She gingerly touches her skin.

I need a bath. Just what I need to help me relax a little–a nice, hot bath.

She turns on the bathtub's hot-water, then sprinkles some aromatic oils into the tub. As the steam rises it fills the room with a soothing scent of fresh magnolia blossoms. She breathes in deeply, letting the soothing fragrance calm her senses. *Ow, every move I make hurts. Maybe some music*?

Before she continues undressing, she goes into her room and peruses the music next to her CD player. Jazz, mostly. She cues up *Kind of Blue.* She pauses and listens to the melodic piano and calming flourishes of Davis' horn and smiles.

Carly winces with each movement it takes to undress, all the while staring at the scars from the stitches and the fading bruises. The telltale signs of contusions around her eyes are a mixture of washed-out purple smeared with yellow. She scowls at the semi-healed, stitched parts of her body, formerly held together with little metal clamps, disdainful of their resemblance to some garish movie monster. She carefully wraps her casted left arm in the plastic bag provided by the hospital, securing it with medical tape.

Just as she carefully steps into the tub, the telephone rings. *Now*? *I'll let the machine pick it up.* She barely hears the voice.

"Carly, this is Robert. Call me, babe."

As she sinks into the tub, the warm water comforts her. She strives to let the tension ease out of her aching body.

Is someone knocking? Startled, *was that the floorboards in the hall creaking?* After a minute Carly realizes she's been holding her breath. She starts to get up and hears more sounds from the kitchen.

Her pulse quickens. Her vision narrows and darkens. Her movements feel slow in an unreal way, like one does in a dream, running away from someone chasing you, who's trying to hurt you, but you can't run fast enough.

She's frozen with fear.

Did the floorboards just creak again, or am I daydreaming?

Her heart races. She struggles to get out of the tub but slips, her weakened left arm failing to support her weight. In a fashion akin to a poorly executed high-jump, she rolls out of the tub with one leg first. Her body hits the hard tile floor, jarring her left arm and painfully pulling at the mostly healed residual line of stitches on her shoulder. *Shit*!

Not like this. I'm not going down without a fight.

She scans the bathroom for a weapon. *My scissors will do.* Struggling to her feet without the aid of her left arm, she grabs the small, pointed scissors out of the medicine cabinet.

With her thinking numb, she turns off the light. *Oh God, I'm naked. Where's my robe*? Attempting to find her robe, she slips on the wet floor. Feeling a sharp pain wrap around her rib cage, Carly fights to breathe. Anger boils up inside her, threatening to drown her.

Not without a fight, you bastard, bring it! *I've been a victim my whole life. No more*! Holding her breath, she strains to remain silent.

"Are you okay in there? Did you fall?" The detective's voice pierces the silence.

Still trembling as her fury-filled adrenaline rush subsides, Carly lets out a huge sigh of relief realizing it's Detective Daugherty.

"I'm fine," she calls back, letting out a big sigh, completely frustrated with herself for over-reacting.

Exasperated, Carly turns on the light, allowing her anxiety ratcheting her pulse to subside, and dries off. After putting on a pair of sweatpants and an old, oversized T-shirt, she walks into the living room.

"Here's your prescription," Detective Daugherty says. "I took the liberty of putting away the food."

"Thank you. How much do I owe you?"

"I left the receipt there. Don't worry about that now, it wasn't much."

"You don't have to stay here. I'm all right."

"Well, it's my job to find out what you remember. I'm hanging around hoping something you see or smell will jog your memory. When you feel better, I thought I could drive you to your jobs and see if anything comes back to you. You get someone to drive you around and look out for you, I get to potentially finish my work. I see this as win-win."

Carly glances around at things in her living room. She walks over to the desk and sees the light flashing on her answering machine. She presses the button.

"Carly, this is Robert. Call me, babe."

She looks at Daugherty. "Before you ask, I don't remember him." Shaking her head, "This can't be the guy who hurt me."

"I don't think anyone would be that stupid. Just so you know, we *have* looked into him. He seems like an okay guy."

Raising her eyebrows, Carly stares incredulously. "Really?"

"We've looked into everyone you know, everyone in your orbit–everyone we're aware of anyhow."

Daugherty steps into the kitchen. "Are you hungry? Let me fix you some soup. No arguing. Just take it easy." He opens a can of chicken noodle soup. "This is good for what ails you. In working with trauma victims over the past few years, I've learned if you have memory loss, looking at photos may help."

"Yes, pictures, I should look at some." Carly walks over to one of the bookcases and pulls out a photo album, with a deep-green cover, embossed with gold filigree. She sits down in the half-moon-shaped window seat in front of the huge bay window, her back up against a pile of pillows. Balancing the album on her lap, the remnants of her healing stitches twinge as she turns the pages, causing her to sway with wooziness. "I think I need to lie down. I don't feel so well."

"Maybe you just need to rest."

As Carly nods off, the last image she sees is of Detective Daugherty covering her with a colorful throw from the back of the couch.

***

Carly wakes up, glances around, disoriented. Detective Daugherty sits on one of her overstuffed leather chairs reading a book.

"Hi," he says, smiling. "Feeling better?"

"Um, I guess. Better. I…I'm a little hungry."

"I'll warm up that soup again."

"Um, how long was I asleep?"

"About two hours. No doubt you needed it." He stands, walks into the kitchen, placing the bowl back in the microwave to warm it up. "Two jobs and a therapist left messages for you on the machine."

"Two jobs?"

"In the course of my work, I told them you were recovering from an unfortunate event."

Detective Daugherty hands Carly the messages.

"Wait, you came into my apartment while I was in the hospital and unconscious?"

"Yes, remember? I mentioned this to you before. It's standard procedure in a situation like this. We have to investigate to minimize any further risk."

Carly looks at the messages. *A therapist*? *Maybe she can help me.* Carly calls her back to see if she can see her soon. "Hi, Dr. Mentes, this is Carly McCulley. I just got out of the hospital and was wondering if I could come see you. Okay, great. 3 o'clock tomorrow afternoon? Thanks, see you then."

"Come here and have some soup."

"Well, thank you for all you've done." Carly carefully sits down and eagerly eats the soup. "This is delicious."

"You're welcome. I'll tell you what, I'll come by tomorrow and pick you up and take you to your appointment. With any luck, some of your memory will have returned, and then hopefully, I'll be able to complete my paperwork."

"You really don't have to, I'll be fine."

"You need someone to take you to your appointment, and you're in no condition to drive. It's no trouble, really."

"Okay. My appointment is at 3 o'clock. Can you come by about 2:30? I'd appreciate it so much."

"My pleasure. See you tomorrow. Remember, you have my number. Call me if you need anything."

Detective Daugherty ducks out the door. Carly rushes over, snaps the deadbolt into place, breathing easier. She rests her forehead on the door, then eases back with anxiety poking her from the shadows of her mind, taunting her with an elusive threat.

She turns, making her way to the kitchen and her soup, glancing over her shoulder to make sure the door is still closed and locked.

CHAPTER SIX

THREATENING PHONE CALL

A ringing phone jolts Carly awake. She drifts back to sleep. The phone rings again. Startled and panicked, fear washing over her, she gets up and staggers into the living room.

I'll let the machine pick it up.

An eerie, unknown male voice whispers, "We have some unfinished business. I'm watching you."

A blanket of dread descends on Carly.

What is going on? I probably should tell the detective about this.

CHAPTER SEVEN

FIRST THERAPY APPOINTMENT

Carly sinks deep into the black leather seat of Detective Daugherty's Charger. If he hadn't picked her up and insisted she go, Carly would've canceled on her therapist. It's going to take a lot of energy and courage to face this unknown specter clouding her mind.

"Thanks for dropping me off. I should be okay," Carly says. "I hope I'm not a burden."

"No way!" Daugherty says. "If you don't mind, I'd like to ask the doc a couple questions, with you present, of course. Then I have a couple errands to run, but I'm gonna come back and escort you home."

Carly sighs. "No, I don't mind, but you really don't have to come back. I can find my way home."

"This is part of my job, and besides, you might remember something." He flashes an impish smile, raising his eyebrows. "No use arguing."

"It's really not necessary. I can take the bus."

"Do you really want to be out on a bus all bruised up with your arm in a sling? Just let me help. Besides, I feel like I'm fulfilling my sworn duty as a civil servant by doing this for you."

Carly sighs, then smiles and nods. “All right. I should be done in about an hour. Thanks.”

“I have an idea. I thought since you’re still recovering, I could take you out to dinner. It’s not a date or anything, but it will be helpful to you. Our talking may help me with my job. This is really selfish on my part.”

Carly looks down and sighs, unsure about the detective’s motives. Caught off guard, she says, “I’m not....” The thought of being out in public, vulnerable, hits her like a kick to the gut. “I’m not sure I’m feeling up to it.”

“It will do you good.”

“No, it’s not my injuries. I’d just feel...I don’t know, I feel worried about who’s out there and wants to hurt me. I guess.”

“I know, but this will be the first step in overcoming that, with me, in a supportive, safe environment.”

“You’re probably right,” Carly says, knowing there’d probably never be a good time to get back out in the world. A sudden sense of dread pierces her at the thought of someone lurking in the shadows.

***

They approach the older one-story brick office building in a large complex of nameless office spaces, set apart only by their numbers. Detective Daugherty parks the car and darts out and around to Carly’s door before she opens it.

"Thank you. I really hate being a burden."

They enter a small waiting room, its walls painted light green. There are several wood-frame chairs with black faux-leather covers lining the walls, abutted by end tables full of magazines and literature for self-help seekers. A muted lamp glows in the far corner.

A bell sits on the ledge in front of a small reception window. Taped to the glass, a sign reads:

> *Please sign in, fill out any paperwork, ring the bell, and wait patiently. Someone will be with you shortly. Thank you.*

Carly takes the clipboard with a single sheet of paper and pen attached, reading the instructions.

"It looks like she wants to find out if I'm depressed. Imagine that," Carly sarcastically muses.

Detective Daugherty raises an eyebrow, cocks his head, shaking it and smiles.

Carly responds to the questions with a sense of duty. Hoping they can somehow jar her memory. She squints a couple of times, hanging her head. After she finishes, she approaches the window, rings the bell, and returns to her chair. "This place seems familiar somehow."

The door opens. Dr. Barbara Mentes, a slight woman with a friendly, weathered face, appears and looks at both Carly and Detective Daugherty. "Hi, Carly. It's good to see you." She looks toward Detective Daugherty. "Hello, I'm Dr. Mentes."

"Hello, I'm Detective John Daugherty, New Brunswick Police Department. I gave Carly a ride and am kind of looking out for her while I'm investigating her recent incident."

"Nice to meet you."

"I have a couple of questions for you relative to that, if you don't mind."

"As far as answering any questions," Dr. Mentes says, "you realize there are doctor–patient confidentiality rules that I must adhere to."

After seeing that no one else is around to overhear, Carly interjects, "It's okay, Dr. Mentes. He's helping me."

"Well, in that case. What are your questions?"

"How long has Ms. McCulley been coming to see you?"

"For about two maybe three years."

"What was she mainly coming to see you for?"

"Depression. I also diagnosed her as having PTSD, schizoid issues and related concerns."

"Did she ever talk to you about someone threatening her or harassing her?"

"If I take your meaning correctly, to my recollection, she did not."

"Did she have any enemies that you know of?"

"No. I believe she's well liked."

"I'd like to get a copy of your file, if I could."

"I will have Carly sign a Release of Information form, but copying the records will take some time. I don't have it available to just photocopy. I'll have my assistant work on that and will call you when it's ready. Do you have a business card?"

"Yes, ma'am." Detective Daugherty reaches in his jacket and pulls out a business card and hands it to Dr. Mentes. "Thank you. Those are all the questions I have for now."

"Carly, the detective can wait out here if you'd like."

"Well, actually, I have a couple errands to run. I'll be back in about an hour to pick Carly up."

***

Carly follows Dr. Mentes through the well-lit hall back to a corner office. Thick, burgundy-colored carpet covers the floor. The walls feature brightly colored paintings with flowers and stairways and open doors. The remainder of the wall space is filled with bookshelves containing hundreds of books. Dr. Mentes' large oak desk resides in one corner, flanked by a black, high-backed leather chair. The opposite corner of the room houses an area filled with toys; Dr. Seuss books adorn a kiddie table surrounded by two child-sized chairs. The requisite diplomas are displayed on one wall. Off to one side of the room are several overstuffed burgundy leather chairs facing each other, including a stretched-out recliner. With mounting trepidation, Carly thinks, *This must be the shrink couch. What am I nervous about? Why am I feeling like this*?

Dr. Mentes makes a sweeping motion. "Pick any seat, Carly."

"Do you want me to lie down?"

"Only if you want to."

"Where do I usually sit?"

"Let's not worry about what you usually do. Just pick a spot you feel comfortable in."

Carly settles into the big, comfy leather chair with her back to the wall, where she can see the door.

Dr. Mentes looks over the form Carly filled out, then up at her. "So, your memory is gone? Why don't we start there, unless there's something else you'd like to talk about?"

Carly hangs her head. "Well, I'm not sure where to begin."

"How about where you have some strong feelings. Is there anything weighing on your mind more than anything else?"

After thinking for a second, Carly asks, "What was I coming to see you for?"

Dr. Mentes pauses. "Like I told the detective, we were working on your feelings that resulted from you experiencing PTSD, as well as some recent losses in your life. We were dealing with your feelings of depression."

Carly stares with no comprehension of how that is her reality, but something stirs inside of her. "PTSD? And–what else did you say to the detective–schizoid issues? Can you tell me more about that diagnosis? What is that related to?"

"I am uncomfortable labeling people, other than when I *have to* for insurance reasons because I don't want you to embrace that label as being part of who you are, as if it's something tangible like your eye color. It's just a way to describe and communicate ideas. Some of your struggles and the issues you are dealing with came from your distant past, and some of it was from recent events."

"Tell me again, how long have I been seeing you?"

"A couple of years. Maybe a bit longer. You don't have memories of any of this, of who you are or what we were working on in our sessions?"

Carly shakes her head. "When I first walked in, I had a glimmer of recognition of your office. I think it was a familiar smell."

"Tell me, do you remember anything? Have you come across anything else anywhere that has triggered any memories? It could even be a sense or a feeling that seems familiar."

"I think I remember how my place smells, and I remembered the year and who was president but not my name or where I live, what I do for a living, or how I ended up in a parking lot beaten up and unconscious."

"What? You were found in a parking lot beaten up and unconscious?" Dr. Mentes' eyes widen and her brow creases with apparent concern. "What happened to you?"

"I was buying a bottle of wine at the corner liquor store. Wow, I hadn't thought about that. I was going somewhere. It's all really fuzzy. Then I woke up in the hospital."

"Can you tell me if you remember anything about the assault, or what you know related to that?"

"Nothing I remember, just what they told me–that two men found me outside at the Fourth Street 7-Eleven.

I had a couple of cracked ribs, cuts over various parts of my body. I had hit my head and was lying unconscious in the parking lot."

Shaking her head, Dr. Mentes queries further, "And this happened when?"

"A few weeks ago, I think. Can you give me more details of why I was seeing you again?"

"Initially when you came to see me, we were working on issues in your marriage. Most recently, I was helping you deal with some losses, and we were working on some issues from your childhood."

"I was married? Losses? What kind of losses?"

"I don't want to give you too much information too soon. It wouldn't be good to just bombard you with information you might not be ready to deal with. What I *will* give you are some pages of the transcribed therapy sessions from past appointments. I want you to read them, for–well, let's call it a type of homework. At the very least, it will inform some of your history. At best, it may precipitate your memories returning.

"All of our sessions are recorded, which I then get transcribed verbatim."

"Verbatim? You mean everything we said in each session is typed out?"

"Correct, word-for-word."

"So you have recordings of all of our therapy sessions?"

"Yes. I find it's a good tool to help my work, when I can go back and review what was actually said in a session."

Nodding, Carly asks, “So, is there anything else I can do or you can do to help me get my memories back?”

“There are lots of things we can try. After head trauma, memories might be recovered spontaneously. It’s not uncommon that events immediately preceding and following head trauma are fuzzy. Eventually you’ll remember more about your life. One day you’ll be doing an ordinary task, and your memories will all come flooding back.

“Right now, I’d like to do some hypnosis therapy, if you are agreeable. Maybe we can get past the immediate roadblock that’s impeding you from remembering.”

“Have I done this before? Is this safe?”

“Yes, we have, and yes, it’s safe,” Dr. Mentes says with a reassuring smile. “It’s just a process to relax you, which attempts to sneak past any defenses in your subconscious that might be preventing you from remembering.”

Carly considers this, as unease bubbles up inside her. *Without this, even as bad as it could be, will I ever be able to recover the details of my life?* “Okay.”

“If it helps, you once told me that you trust me. Please feel that space somewhere inside yourself. I’m here to help.”

“I believe you.” *I think.*

“Okay, sit back, close your eyes, and try to relax. Just focus on your breathing.”

Carly relaxes as Dr. Mentes continues speaking in a soft, soothing voice.

"Take deep, slow, calming breaths, in and out, in and out. Now relax, and imagine yourself walking down a hall and past doors with numbers on them. These are painted numbers, black on white doors or white numbers on black doors, whichever you like."

Carly takes a deep breath and tries to visualize the doors in her head, white numbers gleaming against smooth black wood.

"As you pass the doors you'll relax more and more. As I say the number, you'll pass the door: ten, nine, eight, seven," Dr. Mentes continues. "As you pass the doors, you will feel more and more relaxed. Focus on your breathing, in and out. You're becoming more and more relaxed. Six, five, four. Now you see a stairway, and you start to descend. You can see door number three."

Feeling dizzy, Carly approaches the black door, impossibly darker than the rest, her vision narrows until it floods with darkness. She panics, overwhelmed by a stifling choking feeling that leaves her confused and paralyzed with anxiety. *What the hell? Why can't I breathe? What am I afraid of?*

Her feelings build to a boiling point and she bolts up, unable to bear it any longer, blurting out, "I can't...I don't want to do this right now." Carly hangs her head, covering her face with her palms, pausing to regain her composure. "I'm really tired. Maybe reading your notes at home is something I can handle."

After pausing a moment, Dr. Mentes says, "Okay. What happened?"

"I don't know. I was walking toward the door, down the stairs, and kinda...freaked out, I guess. I couldn't breathe. I dunno. I felt like I was choking."

"My intention was to help you feel relaxed and safe. I was trying to bypass your defenses, into your subconscious, into your memories," Dr. Mentes clarifies with a sympathetic smile. "Let me go make those copies of our transcribed session notes for you."

Carly nods.

"Before I get those copies–I want to explain, going through therapy, even under normal circumstances, is a lot of work. We essentially uncover old wounds–things that have been difficult to resolve. It can be unsettling and even painful to delve in and stir up long-resting memories. In your case, you are also having to deal with present trauma. I think your reaction while under hypnosis is completely normal given what you've experienced recently."

"I categorize my patients into three types," Dr Mentes continues. "The first type are coming to see me because they have to. Someone else is coercing them. A second type may see their issues, but then have an unending number of excuses for their problems. They tend to cast blame outside of themselves and end up not taking responsibility for their lives. The third type of patient honestly wants to learn, face their truth, and grow past it–this is where I see you, Carly." Dr. Mentes smiles. "I have seen a strength of courage in you to face the truth in your life that I have not seen in many of my patients. I am confident that you will be able to meet these current challenges well."

She pauses. "When would you like to come in again?"

Shaking her head, Carly can't help but think: *Not for a damn long time. I don't want to do this right now.* "I don't know, this was a lot."

"Okay. Maybe this was too much too soon, and you're not ready to uncover what happened yet."

Carly nods. Dr. Mentes stands up, collects a few pages from the file on her desk and takes them to a small copier in the corner.

"What about Thursday?" Dr. Mentes asks, smiling. "Along with reading some of our transcribed session notes, it may help you recover your memories if you look at some old photos. Relax, have a glass of wine, listen to some good music, something that makes you happy. Spray some of your favorite perfume around. And remember to breathe. Many times, when we are stressed, we hold our breath without realizing it."

Dr. Mentes places the fresh copies of the pages of transcript into a manila folder and hands it to Carly. "Also, I want to suggest you write out anything that comes to mind that you feel strongly about. Bring those pages with you next time."

"Okay, hopefully I'll be feeling better by then," Carly says, doubting her words. "Thank you, Doctor."

CHAPTER EIGHT

DINNER WITH DETECTIVE DAUGHERTY

Carly sees Detective Daugherty sitting in the waiting room as she exits the doctor's office. She smiles, surprisingly reassured at his presence. "I was half expecting you not to be here."

"To protect and to serve. I was an Eagle Scout, you know. This is one of the first things you learn–dependability. Where would you like to go to eat? Again, this is not a date, but like we discussed, you have to eat."

"Um, I–let me think." Carly sighs.

"No pressure."

Carly, still numb from her therapy session, says, "Thank you for this. I don't know. What do you feel like?"

"Well, I've been hungry for Chinese food. I know a great place. It's quiet, and they have amazing egg drop soup and fried wontons."

"I don't know what kinda company I'll be."

"It's fine. This is something I'm doing for *you*. Under the circumstances, I'm not expecting…um, don't worry, just be yourself, whatever *that* is. Okay?"

Carly feels grateful for the company. She's tired of being alone with her thoughts and too much in her head. She smiles. "Thank you." *He is a good and kind man.*

***

They pull up to a Chinese restaurant whose entrance is embossed with an intricately carved image of a bonsai tree. Dozens of jade-green, leather-covered booths encircle the interior of the restaurant, while the center houses ten white linen-covered diagonally placed tables. In the middle of each table, a single glass-covered candle sits next to an aromatic lotus bloom floating in a small ornate bowl filled with water.

As they wait at the front to be seated, Carly notices a huge glass-partitioned case containing several types of exotic fish on ice, alongside ducks' feet, crab, and other foods she can't easily identify.

The gentle aroma of fried egg rolls wafts through the air as they are greeted by a diminutive woman wearing a green satin, mandarin-collared dress, painted with what appears to be scenes of bamboo and cherry blossoms. She leads them to their seats. After handing them each a menu, she states, "Your server will be with you shortly to take your order."

"How was your appointment? You seemed a little upset when you walked out."

"Yeah, this is all kinda...." She pauses, trying to find the right word. "Rough. Talking to my therapist just made me feel worse. I thought it would help, but...I just feel worse," she says, shaking her head.

A young waitress in black satin slacks and a white blouse approaches their table, her order pad in hand.

"My name is Liang. I'll be your server this evening. Can I get you something to drink?"

"We'd like a bottle of plum wine and two glasses of water."

With a polite smile, the server says, "Very good. Are you ready to order?"

Carly nods. "I'd like the cashew chicken with steamed rice."

Daugherty says, "I'll have the egg drop soup. Could I get some chicken fried rice and two of your special egg rolls?"

"Anything else?"

They both shake their heads no and smile.

"Okay, I'll be right back with your wine."

After a slight pause, Detective Daugherty asks, "About your appointment. Do you wanna talk about it?"

Carly takes a big breath and looks down at the floor. "I don't know. The doctor was telling me generally what we were working on. It's just…I don't know. I was trying to explain what happened, and she used hypnosis therapy to help me relax and look into my subconscious for answers, but it seemed like the opposite happened. I just felt more anxious."

"I haven't experienced anything exactly like this, but I can imagine. I think you have to give it time. Your memories *will* come back–some things just can't be rushed. I get how frustrating this must be for you, especially having to face it all alone. This may sound trite, but just remember to breathe."

Carly sighs. "I just feel so–so helpless and not in control."

Daugherty smiles and pats her wrist, which she pulls away.

"Sorry, I just…." Carly glances away, unable to look the detective in the eye.

"Don't worry. I get it," Daugherty says, seeming to disregard the rebuff.

The server comes up with the wine and two glasses and pours some for each of them.

"Thank you." Daugherty smiles.

Carly drinks some of the wine, savoring the sweet taste, wishing to end some of the pain overwhelming her.

"So, how do you like the wine?" Daugherty asks.

"It's delicious." Carly's spirit calms after a couple more sips. "Good choice."

"I'm normally a beer drinker. This is a nice change. May I ask you a question?"

"Sure."

"Do you remember anything from your past?"

"Well, I–it's odd, because I have kind of what seems like a fuzzy sense of myself but nothing specific. I can be going along, then all of a sudden, I remember, oh yeah, I like chocolate. It just happens. I remember something kinda suddenly. It seems to just pop into my mind. Like I remembered I'm an artist, but I don't remember how I got into that. I was trying to remember some art classes or something. I seem to remember how to paint, almost like it's something I know, but don't know *how* I know it, if that makes sense?"

"Yes, I think I understand. Your memory is hazy about who you are. You remember some things, but you don't remember how you know those things. I get it. But you don't remember anything, like high school or college?"

"No. Well, I haven't really thought about that, and so far, looking at old pictures hasn't triggered any memories. I was thinking maybe if I visit where I work. That might help some memories return. And, I feel a bit stir-crazy being laid up for so long.

"Oh, and I almost forgot. Someone called and left a creepy message on my machine last night in the middle of the night."

"Was it a man or a woman?"

"A man."

"What did he say?"

"He said something like, we had unfinished business and he was watching me. That was it." An uneasy dread washes over Carly as she recounts this. Somehow sharing this makes it feel menacing to her.

"Okay, tomorrow, before you go visit work, I would like you to come down to the station and speak with one of our detectives, Jim Franklin."

"Is there any specific reason?"

"No, this is pretty much routine. He just wants to ask a few questions about what happened to you. Please bring your answering machine."

"My answering machine?"

"Yes. We would like to copy the message from it and have our guys analyze that."

"Sure thing. Okay. Sounds like a plan."

The waitress comes up with their food, moving everything around and placing the various dishes on their table. Carly bumps Detective Daugherty's arm a couple times. *I feel safe with him.*

"This looks yummy. I'm hungrier than I thought."

"This smells wonderful. I love the smell of chicken fried rice and ginger, or maybe I'm just enjoying this wine," Daugherty says with a sheepish grin. "Or the company, or both."

After they finish eating, Detective Daugherty pays. As they walk outside, he asks, "Are you chilly?"

"Maybe a little."

He takes off his coat and puts it around Carly's shoulders. "Thanks." *How thoughtful.*

Detective Daugherty drives Carly home. She watches people and cars blur past. Envy creeps into Carly's mind at the unfairness that she doesn't remember most anything. She considers, *that woman knows where she got her dog, remembers the joy of meeting it for the first time and every moment since. Those boys playing basketball remember learning to play and the many hours of repeatedly tossing the ball toward the rim. The elderly couple sitting together holding hands at the bus stop remember where they met and their first date.*

The car stops. Detective Daugherty gets out, hurriedly circles the rear of the car, and opens the passenger door. He takes Carly's hand and helps her out of the car, escorting her to the door.

She removes the coat from her shoulders. “Here’s your coat back, Detective. Thank you.”

“Okay, well, you have my number. Call if any memories come back, or if you need anything or just want to talk or whatever. Good night, Ms. McCulley.”

An uneasy dread invades Carly’s mind, as she anticipates her trip to the police station. She is further disquieted by the acute awareness of her lack of memory and the detective’s seeming overattentiveness.

CHAPTER NINE

QUESTIONING

Carly parks in the large lot a block from the police station. She walks to the aging six-story, red-brick building, up the few steps, through the glass-paneled doors, and across the foyer to the front desk. Maple-stained paneling covers the waiting area, a stylistic relic of decades past. A sharply dressed police officer sits at the front desk behind a solitary glass-free window.

Carly says, "I'm here to see Detective Daugherty from the Special Victims Unit."

"What's your name?"

"Carly McCulley. He is expecting me." She suddenly feels apprehensive for no apparent cause.

"I'll let him know you're here. Attach this visitor badge to your jacket and take a seat."

"Thank you."

Detective Daugherty emerges from one of the hallways leading off the waiting area. He extends his hand to Carly, smiling. "How are ya doing? Follow me."

"Well, honestly, nervous."

As they walk up to a small, windowless conference room, Carly observes a forty-something year old man with dark, thinning hair and a decent-sized paunch. He approaches and extends his hand.

Detective Daugherty says, "Jim, this is Carly McCulley. Carly, this is Jim Franklin. He has a few questions for you."

"Hi, Ms. McCulley."

Carly takes his hand. "What kind of questions?"

Jim gestures, pointing toward Daugherty. "I don't know how much Detective Daugherty has told you. I'm a homicide detective here at New Brunswick."

Carly sits at the end of the table, observing the detectives. "He told me a little."

"We're working a case–tracking someone we refer to as The Tailor." Taking a deep breath, Jim states, "I don't want to alarm you, but some of the marks on your wrists and the various cuts you sustained during the assault you recently endured resemble some of the wounds we've seen on the victims in our case. We think maybe, just maybe, you're someone who got away."

Victims? Adrenaline stabs at Carly's core, as a wave of dread crashes over her, Carly's eyes widen and her eyebrows raise. "What?!"

"I'm not saying anything definitive, yet."

Stunned and shaken, Carly continues to question the officers. "There are 'victims,' as in more than one? And you think this guy is after me? Why?"

"Like I said, we are not certain about this. I don't want to get too deep into the weeds of this investigation if it has nothing to do with you and your situation. I have a couple questions, if you don't mind. What do you remember prior to waking up in the hospital?"

"Well, everything's fuzzy. I think I remember going to buy a bottle of wine, but not a whole lot after that until I woke up the other day."

"Do you remember if you were going to that 7-Eleven where you were found?"

Shaking her head Carly responds, "I don't think I ever shop there. Those stores usually have high prices, and it's not close to where I live."

Detective Franklin aggressively presses, "You don't remember where you were or what you were doing or who you were with the Friday night prior to ending up in that parking lot," all the while staring directly at Carly.

Carly shakes her head, looking down at her hands. "I've had some memories come back recently, but it has nothing to do with what you just asked."

"So, you don't remember how you got to the parking lot at the 7-Eleven or how you got in the condition you were in?" Detective Franklin pauses, looking past Carly momentarily. "We think the guy who's left you a message while you were in the hospital, and the most recent one, may be The Tailor, so we put a protective surveillance detail on you. Did you bring your answering machine?"

Carly retrieves the machine from inside her big leather bag. "Yes, here it is. You think the killer you are looking for left a message for me while I was in the hospital?"

"That is what we want to determine. Do I have your permission to listen to this and make a copy of the recordings?"

"Sure." Carly is suddenly overwhelmed with an uneasy foreboding deep in the pit of her stomach.

Frankling turns, pointing and motioning with his finger at Daugherty. "John, why don't you come with me while I do that?"

"I can't believe this. Why would a killer be leaving me messages? If he knows who I am, why hasn't he done something more?" Carly queries, shaking her head.

"If this is The Tailor, we're concerned he'll try to get to you again and finish what he started."

"What?!" Anger replaces Carly's dread as adrenaline rushes through her, all the while she stares down Detective Daugherty. "Why didn't you tell me this?"

"We didn't know anything for certain, and really still don't," Daugherty states, glaring at Detective Franklin.

"You think he's gonna try again? Why hasn't he done something?" Carly repeats her question, shaking her head, as anger wells up inside her.

"Most likely because he doesn't know where you live," Jim suggests. "We're going to keep surveillance in place on you on an undercover basis for the time being. You shouldn't even realize they're watching. Again, if you remember anything more, let us know right away."

Detective Daugherty says, "I'll be keeping watch as well."

"What about tapping my phone?" Carly asks.

"We can do that, but we need your authorization."

"Authorized."

"Well," Daugherty says, "we also need a judge's approval."

Carly covers her face with her hands, dismayed, shaking her head. "Why did you tell me this now?"

"I'm sorry," Daugherty says, reaching across the table, taking one of her hands. "I didn't want to alarm you, but ultimately, we had to inform you and let you know what's going on. I'd hoped you'd be somewhat comforted knowing we have had officers keeping an eye on you. Stay here, we'll be right back. We're going upstairs and will put together the paperwork to start the wiretap."

Carly nods, feeling betrayed and angry. She wishes Daugherty had told her sooner.

***

After about 30 minutes, Detective Daugherty and Detective Franklin return. The latter hands Carly her answering machine.

"Okay, so what do I do now? Go on as if everything is normal? I have some questions."

"We *cannot* discuss this." Detective Franklin emphatically states.

"Why would he be after *me*?"

"Sorry, Ms. McCulley," Franklin says, a hardened edge to his voice. "We cannot discuss any more details of an open investigation with you or anyone–anything more could put you in danger."

"Yeah, but if this guy's after me, I think I should know why or at least as much as possible about all this."

"You can't remember anything?" Detective Franklin prods again. "You don't know why someone would want to harm you?"

Daugherty steps in between them. "Jim, I don't think..."

"Not now, Daugherty."

Franklin turns to Carly. "I just have to wonder why this guy is after you. The one thing that most of this guy's victims have in common is that they had children who died under suspicious circumstances."

Upon hearing this, Carly is overcome with hot anger and intense sadness, mustering all her willpower not to burst out crying. "I need to go."

Detective Franklin breathes in deeply, slapping both hands on the table face down and leaning back in his chair. "Well, I have no more questions for you right now."

"Come on, I'll walk you out." Detective Daugherty gently takes Carly's arm.

They weave their way down the hall, the stairs, the entryway, and outside. Carly has never felt so glad to have a breath of fresh air.

"Sorry for that." Daugherty says. "He didn't tell me what he was planning to ask to you, or that he'd talk to you with that tone."

After barely acknowledging the detective's comments with a nod, and with intense anger boiling just under the surface of her thoughts mixed with mind-numbing confusion, Carly gets into her car and quietly sobs, feeling smothered by the weight of this new and unwelcome knowledge.

CHAPTER TEN

NIGHTMARE AND SESSION NOTES

Carly struggles and feels as if a heavy weight crushes her chest. She realizes she's tied up and gagging from something stuck in her mouth. She lies spread-eagle on a bed or the floor, a terrible pain in her side. Her arms are stretched out. An ominous presence looms close. She senses people are coming, chasing her. They want to kill her.

If I can just get away and find dad, I'll be okay.

Oh no, I can't get up. Am I being held down or tied down? There are people all around me holding me down. Everything is black. I can't breathe.

Panic sets in. Carly is paralyzed with fear.

Carly bolts up in bed, trembling and sweating. *Just a nightmare*. Panicked, she feels as though someone is in the room. She gets up and flips on a lamp, then hangs a scarf over it to mute its unwelcome brightness. The clock reads 3:07 a.m. She feels alone and helpless.

As she turns around in the near darkness, suddenly glimpsing her reflection in the mirror, her heart races. *Goddammit*! *What the hell is wrong with me*?

Carly climbs back into bed, yet sleep evades her just as her memories have. Finally surrendering to the insomnia, she gets up, goes into the living room, and switches on the reading light behind her comfy, overstuffed chair. She moves a couple pillows to the floor and gingerly sits down, opening the file that Dr. Mentes gave her.

Excerpt of therapy session notes:
Dr. Mentes: February 27, 1997: Patient, Carly McCulley–Continuing Diagnosis–schizoid Personality issues, PTSD, dysthymia, insomnia, nightmares. Will try hypnosis to uncover why she is angry and why she has turned that in on herself, leading to her depression.
Verbatim transcription of therapy session this date follows:
Dr. Mentes: Let's talk about the recurring dream you keep having. Describe it to me.
Carly: Well, the dream is basically people chasing me and trying to kill me.
Dr. Mentes: Is it day or night?
Carly: Sometimes it's day, sometimes night.
Dr. Mentes: Do you know where you are?
Carly: Yes, in my house where I was born.
Dr. Mentes: Do you know who was chasing you?
Carly: No, I don't think so. I just get the sense it is people.
Dr. Mentes: Has the dream changed? Is it always the same, or does it differ?

Carly: It's kinda gotten more specific. I keep thinking if I could just find my dad, I'd be okay, but I don't see him or sense him anywhere.
Dr. Mentes: Describe how the dream has changed.
Carly: I'd be running and trying to get away and had a sense of people chasing me. Later, people were chasing me down a hall, and I ran into a bathroom, and the door fell on me.

Then I had a dream I was running down a street, and a man was chasing me with a gun. I run inside an apartment building, and there's a glass door separating us, and I can see him staring at me. I back away, frightened, and wake up terrified.
Dr. Mentes: Are you always being chased? Is this a consistent theme?
Carly: Yes. The most recent one was me running down the street and turning into a bar, then going to the back room and trying to hide under a mattress. The man who chases me follows and sits on the bed. I'm so scared I can't move. The man leans over to stare at me. He's pointing a gun at me. I wake up so frightened I can't breathe.

Upon reading this, an elusive but persistent dread rises inside of Carly.

Dr. Mentes: Did you see the man this last time?
Carly: Yes, the last one was the one I just described.
Dr. Mentes: I'm going to ask you some questions to kind of get you to become objects in your dream, and I want you to tell me what the different parts of your dream mean to you. Does that make sense? As an example, if there is a chair in the dream, try to sense what the chair is doing in the dream.
Carly: Um, why?
Dr. Mentes: It's a Gestalt therapy technique, of sorts. This will potentially help uncover the meanings behind the elements of the things in your dreams. We can get an idea of what the dream means to you by getting a sense of how the items in the dream relate to you. Does that make sense? If not, don't worry, just respond to my questions. Don't think about the questions too much. Just answer instinctively.
Carly: Yes...um...okay.
Dr. Mentes: Who are the people?
Carly: I dunno.
Dr. Mentes: What does the mattress represent to you?
Carly: It's protecting me.
Dr. Mentes: What does the gun represent to you?
Carly: Um...I dunno.
Dr. Mentes: Is the man using the gun to shoot at you?

Carly: Maybe. I'm really uncomfortable thinking this, but the first thing I thought of was a penis. I don't even want to think this, let alone say it.

Disgust boils up from Carly's gut and chokes her as she struggles to process what she is reading.

Dr. Mentes: Are you okay? How are you feeling?
Carly: I feel kinda spacey. It's hard to describe. It's kinda like I'm not really here anymore. Kinda like I'm detached from myself and floating up behind myself.
Dr. Mentes: Okay. Let's bring you back. You did a lot of good work today.

Carly starts to feel spacey after she reads these words. She considers the cause. *What just happened to me*? She puts down the session notes, her mind races as she considers what she has just read.

Desiring to put what she read out of her mind, Carly directs her thoughts toward uncovering clues about her past, and walks over to search through her old desk that reveals the contents of the numerous pigeonholes only after the top is rolled back. *Maybe there will be something, anything in here that might help me remember. This desk was a wedding present from my dad. That's a memory. Where is my husband?*

Approaching the desk, she notices the answering-machine light flashing. She presses the button. "Hey, Carly, this is Robert. Where are you? Call me." *What a comforting voice. Maybe I'll call him tomorrow. But who's Robert anyway? What if he's the one who hurt me? Can I trust him?*

Carly searches through the desk's crevices looking for some scrap of information, but she finds nothing that sheds any light on anything. This desk is as devoid of answers as is her mind.

I need to talk to someone who remembers me. Carly looks through her index of phones numbers and stops at her cousin's phone number, sensing some type of familiarity. *I'll call her tomorrow.*

Maybe something in the bedroom will trigger something.

Carly returns to her bedroom and searches the bookshelves for a book about dreams or recovering memories. As she looks around, for the first time she realizes that the pictures are all facedown. She picks up one of the picture frames. There are several pictures of a happy family with a young, fair-haired girl and a handsome, 30ish-year-old man with dark hair and warm, blue eyes. She gazes at the pictures, not remembering them. *Is this my husband? Who is the little girl? Where are they?* In the background of her mind a subtle foreboding melody plays, stirring something deep within her soul. Sadness? Anxiety? Longing? Anger?

She walks back out to her desk and sits in the burgundy, high-backed leather chair, and turns on the computer attempting to find some information related to what had happened to her. She does a search in the *New*

Brunswick Times. Let's see, when did this happen? About three weeks ago. She finds an article:

> Local girl found beaten, stabbed and unconscious in the 4th Street 7-Eleven parking lot. Anyone who has any knowledge or any information surrounding this event, please call New Brunswick Police.

Carly feels as if she's reading about a stranger. *Why don't I feel anything*? *Why don't I remember*? *What's wrong with me*?

Feeling numb, she goes over to the bay window and out of habit attempts to curl up in a semi-fetal position with her legs pulled up against her bottom, but a tug of pain from her mostly healed wounds prevents it. She takes a pillow and leans up against the glass instead. As she twirls her hair, she senses a memory of a woman's voice telling her to stop it or her hair will fall out. She continues the twirling in defiance. Was that her mother's voice, or perhaps someone else? Another memory? *I wonder who that is, where she lives, or if she's still alive.*

Her memory flickers like the streetlight outside her window. She continues staring, trying to find answers to questions she hasn't thought to ask.

Even though it's night, Carly sees the sky darkening. *A storm is coming*. She cranks open the window. The warm super charged wind caresses her skin. With a sudden crack of lightning, her reflection flashes on the window, startling her, sending a piercing surge of adrenaline-soaked dread through her body. She gasps. *Jesus Christ, calm down.* For a split second, she feels someone is watching her. She again attempts to pull her legs close to her body to hug them. Letting out a sigh, she realizes she was holding her breath.

CHAPTER ELEVEN

ATTEMPT AT NORMALCY

Still winged and feeling stir-crazy, Carly cleans up and decides to make a couple phone calls. First up, her cousin.

"Hello, I'm trying to reach Sarah Fisher."

"She's not here now. Can I take a message?"

"Sure, this is her cousin Carly. I believe she has my number."

"Okay, I'll let her know you called."

Taking a big breath, Carly dials Robert. With her heart racing, she hangs up. *Maybe going to my jobs will help me remember something.*

***

Carly drives to the MedX address and parks. It's located in a line of white garages converted to office space with normal-sized doors in the middle of larger garage doors.

She walks up to the now-unfamiliar black, stainless-steel door with the large *F* stenciled on it. As she enters the small, musty-smelling reception area with its drab green walls she sees a young blond girl at the front desk. Nervous about what she'll say, Carly glances at the empty chairs spread around one side of the room and the old *People* magazines on the coffee table.

"Hi, I'm–"

"Carly!" the girl shrieks. "Girl, come here. Let me give you a hug." She wraps Carly in her arms and squeezes.

Carly feigns a smile, and groans.

"Sweetie, if there's anything I can do or anything you need, just let me know." The girl excitedly fusses over Carly. "A cop came by and asked a lot of questions. He said you were in the hospital and wouldn't be able to work for a while. We were all so worried."

Carly grits her teeth, already feeling a bit overwhelmed. "When I woke up, my memory was gone."

"Oh, so you don't remember me? You're not in any trouble, are you? We read about you in the news. I'm so glad you're doing better." The girl pauses. "You *are* better, right?"

"Not really. I don't remember, um…."

"So, you don't remember anything? Oh, gosh. Well, my name is Danielle. You called me Dani. Let me take you back and show you around and get you reacquainted with everyone."

"I was kinda hoping coming here would maybe trigger something, you know, in my memory."

"Follow me, sweetie. Girls, look who's here!"

The pale-lavender room they enter is covered with wall-to-wall electric typewriters located in faux-wood-colored carrels crowded next to one another. An island of four computers facing each other occupies the center of the room. Upon hearing Dani's excited announcement, a multitude of ladies crowd around Carly, overwhelming her in an excited ruckus.

"Carly, we're so happy you're doing better!"

"Hurry and get better and come back, we need you!"

"Let me see you. What happened?"

"Can I sign your cast?" One woman takes Carly's casted arm and writes, *Get well soon, girl. Love you, Maggie!*

A thin woman with bobbed, brunette hair swoops in and saves her from the commotion. "Give her some space, ladies," she says in a caring tone. "Come on, hun, come with me. How are you feeling? What happened? Do you remember anything? I'm so sorry."

"Well, I don't remember who I am. It's kinda weird. I remember some things, but I don't remember you or this place. I didn't remember my apartment. But it kinda smells familiar. I remember I like chocolate."

The woman laughs, and Carly cracks a grin.

"How frustrating! By the way, I'm the office manager, Marsha. I can take you around and introduce you to everyone and show you where you sit. Maybe that'll help."

Marsha leads Carly around the floor. "This is Kendra and Susan and Maggie, she signed your cast, and Henry and Kinsey."

Carly smiles and nods at everyone, who respond in kind.

"This is where you sit when you're here at work."

"What did I do here?"

"You transcribe reports for the New Brunswick Probation Department. You're very good at it too."

"Will you tell me a bit more about these reports?"

"Well, if a crime is committed, a probation officer interviews the person who committed the crime to get his side of the events. The officer pulls the prior arrest record if there is one. Then they interview the arresting police officers for details of the crime and arrest. In addition, they interview witnesses, neighbors, employers and family members of the person who was arrested. All of this information goes into the probation report that is given to the judge, with the purpose of providing comprehensive details of the situation, for an informed decision of whether or not the person should be given diversion, probation, community service, or be sent to jail should they be found guilty at trial."

"How long have I been working here?"

"A little over...um, almost two years, I guess? Or maybe a bit more. I'd have to check. You're one of my best workers."

I don't remember anyone. The thought strikes a chord of sadness. She senses a slight familiarity, nothing more.

A couple people come up to sign her cast and give her a hug before she leaves.

"I'm feeling really worn out. I need to get going. Thank you all for your kindness. I'm hoping to get better and get back here as soon as I'm able," Carly says, smiling as she exits.

***

Carly arrives at her apartment to a ringing telephone. Before she reaches it, the answering machine clicks on. She hears Robert's husky voice. "Hey, babe, it's Robert."

With trepidation, Carly picks up the call. "Hi, Robert. Um, this is Carly. I know you've left a couple messages. I just got home and was just–"

"How are ya, babe? I've been concerned about you. A police officer called me and asked me some questions, but he wouldn't give me any details."

"Well, I had a bit of an accident and lost my memory."

"Whoa, an accident? What kind of accident? In your car? Is there anything you need, anything I can do?"

"Um, I was wondering if we could get together for coffee or something."

"Sure, anything for you. Anything I can do to help."

"I have some questions. I feel kinda like these are stupid questions, but are we, like, dating or something?" Carly asks, feeling awkward, awash with shame.

"Wow, you don't remember us? You don't remember me?"

"Nope, nothing."

"Yes, we like each other. We're what you always termed 'friends with benefits.' I've always thought of us as more." Robert pauses for a moment. "It'd be better if we got together and talked. How about lunch? We could go to your favorite sandwich bistro down on Sixth,

Malone's. How about we meet there, say, 1:30-ish to avoid the lunch bunch?"

"Wait, how will I know you?"

"Just look for the handsome guy with dark hair and blue eyes. Anyhow, I think you'll know me when you see me," Robert states with a devilish tone. "Can't wait to see ya. Don't worry…*I know you*."

Carly feels heat rise in her cheeks, embarrassment coursing through her as Robert's last words reverberate inside her, shaking her as her pulse quickens.

Carly looks around the living room.

Empty.

She peers through the peephole into the hallway.

Empty.

If she's going to uncover her former life, regain her identity, she can't hide in her apartment forever.

She fixates on an unavoidable question: *Did Robert attack me? Detective Daugherty said he thought Robert was okay. I probably shouldn't worry.*

CHAPTER TWELVE

CARLY VISITS HER OTHER JOB

Feeling energized but wary, Carly realizes her other part-time job is near Malone's and decides to take the bus to go there prior to lunch with Robert. Carly glances at the paper in her hand and feels a sense of loss at the now-unfamiliar address: *4701 Dupont Drive, New Brunswick.*

The bus jars, startling her. She surveys the passengers, all engrossed in their own affairs.

A wave of anxiety washes over Carly as she considers her visit to her job and her lunch with Robert.

The bus rumbles to a halt at a dilapidated shelter alongside the stop. Carly rises, glances over the passengers. No one stands. A man glances up at her just long enough to look her in the eye, then back down at his book. Her pulse skyrockets with suspicion. She eases down the narrow aisle, moving slowly, the residual pull of the now-healed injuries tug at her side, engendering an elusive dread, with each step echoing the attack in a veiled part of her memory.

With a glance back down the length of the bus, she calms, seeing no one following. She steps out onto the sidewalk.

This must be the place. The address matches a rundown strip mall. Gang insignia sprayed across the brick walls brings an unlikely sense of something familiar. *Well, that's a good sign.*

She approaches the door corresponding to the address on the piece of paper still clutched in her hand. A scarred bronze nameplate reads *Elite Investigations, David Shank*. The name fails to register. She checks the address again. Carly starts to knock but decides just to walk in. *This place seems kinda messy. Wonder what I did here*?

Upon entering, the smell of Grey Flannel aftershave comforts Carly. She notices several desks press up against the walls of the small four-room office area, separated by six-foot-high cubicle dividers. On each desk is a computer, telephone, and inboxes holding numerous manila folders with names marked in black marker across the top.

A tall man sporting unkempt brown hair, his rigid shoulders hidden in a well-worn tweed jacket, strolls in from the back of the office. "Carly! Oh, wow. How are you? Are you okay? When will you be able to come back and help me out here?"

"Um, well–"

"See?" He points to one of the desks, the inbox piled high with folders and papers. "Business is booming. I need you."

Carly raises her casted arm. “Until this is off, I doubt I’ll be much help. I just came in because I was hoping that coming here–you know, someplace familiar–would help get some memories back.”

“Your memories?”

“Yeah. I don’t remember who I am, or much else, really.”

“Well, since you lost your memory, my name’s David. You call me Dave.”

Carly laughs, extends a hand, which Dave shakes. “Nice to meet you, again.”

“Someone stopped by last week, a detective, and said you’d be out for a while. The officer asked about you and what you did and what Elite does. I told him you were a model employee, friendly, punctual and a good worker. I gave you a glowing review.”

“Punctual?” Carly chuckles. “Um, thanks.” She senses a caring comradery with Dave, a feeling, even if nothing specific.

“What happened to you? I mean, if you wanna talk about it.”

“Did we, or I–what did I do here? Was I working on any kind of investigation before this happened? Can you show me?”

“Sure thing.” Dave walks over to the desk he identified as Carly’s.

“This is where I sit? This is my workstation?”

Dave nods. He rifles through the piles of folders. “Here are a couple files you were working on that involved investigation. Nothing too dire, just a workers’ comp sub rosa review and a divorce case transcription. Nothing more sinister or juicy than that, at least that I'm aware of." He hands Carly the set of files.

"Not sure what else you were working on," he continues with a shrug. "Peggy isn't here, or we could get her to pull your logs. You mostly transcribe investigators' reports and do some research and minor investigation stuff for me, but nothing dangerous. We don't deal a lot with the criminal element. We just do basic insurance investigation, cheating spouses and lost people and such."

"Have I gotten any phone calls here from anyone you don't recognize or from anyone asking questions about me?"

"Like I said, just the cop."

Carly nods.

"Do you have any idea what happened to you?" Dave asks.

"Not really. Like I said, most of my memory seems to be gone. It's hard to explain."

"Has seeing anything here helped?"

"Other than a vague sense of you and our working friendship, not really."

"Well, anything I can do, let me know, okay? Just call me."

"Okay."

"No pressure. I just want you to know I need you."

"Okay. I'll let you know when I can return."

"Really, anything you need, just ask. Promise me?"

"Okay. Thanks, David…Dave."

Carly steps through the door and back to the sidewalk, checking up and down the street for anyone with an eye on her. The feeling that she's a burden weighs her down, and a sense of shame floods through her. She'd made little progress with this visit–far less than she'd hoped.

CHAPTER THIRTEEN

COFFEE WITH ROBERT

Carly steps out of the cab in front of Malone's, an old, brick-trimmed, rustic Irish pub that would be right at home in County Cork. She hesitates. Ivy covers the front, growing almost to the rooftop, giving the building a homey artistic feel. The day's specials are listed on a chalkboard standing like a crier by the entrance door.

The welcoming aroma of fried food, warm bread, and freshly brewed coffee entices Carly as she opens the door. She squints upon entering. As her eyes adjust to the dark, she notices rich, mahogany furniture and appointments that fill the pub. The bar extends along one side of the room, backed by a dimly lit mirror dotted with the requisite signs, beer taps, and bottles of assorted spirits. The dark forest-green carpet is plush but well-worn. *This place seems familiar*.

Carly glances over the room for someone who might be Robert. Several people turn to look at her as she enters. Her eyes meet with one man who fits the description of Robert, handsome with blue eyes. Her guarded look lingers on him. He smiles, looks at her arm in the sling, and turns away.

A man approaches from the back of the bistro. He's tall–much taller than Carly–and muscular, clean-cut with dark-brown hair and blue eyes that seem to twinkle. She's struck by a piercing feeling deep inside, an excitement that seems familiar, yet new and alluring.

"Carly!" Robert reaches out and greets her with a protective hug. "You weren't kidding, were you? What happened?"

As Robert touches her, a bolt of electricity courses through her, leaving her stunned, her knees weak. She leans on Robert for support and tries to say something. Time has slowed. She stares at Robert and blinks. "Um...I...."

"You okay? Here, let's go sit down."

"Yeah."

"You really don't remember me? Okay, you're gonna have to trust me," he says with a big smile. "Our booth is back here in the corner."

Supported by Robert's arm, Carly ambles alongside him to a circular booth covered in dark burgundy leather.

Carly slides in, and Robert scoots next to her. She continues to stare. "Sorry. Give me a minute." She feels shaken. Excitement stirring inside her makes it difficult to form thoughts, much less say anything coherent. A jumble of feelings, like a river rushing through her body, overwhelm her. "Maybe you can tell me about you, about us." Carly pauses hoping to regain her composure. "Our relationship."

"Where do I start?"

"The beginning?"

"Well, my name is Robert Hoy."

"How'd we meet? When was it?"

"We met in an art class. A figure-drawing class. Our teacher used to play this awesome music while we created our art. There was one song that will forever be etched in my mind and connected to you: 'Possession,' by Sarah McLachlan. I watched you for a long time. You were so into your work, kind of oblivious to anything going on around you, except your process. A group of us went out for drinks after class one night."

Robert looks into Carly's eyes, smiling. "We had so much chemistry and after a short adjustment, you and I just clicked. Neither of us believed in happily ever after, nor were we interested in it. We both had histories and baggage and just wanted to seize the day. We're a little more than that now. I guess you could say we're very, *very* good friends with benefits."

Their waitress, a perky, thirty-something redhead in a white T-shirt, dark shorts, and little white apron walks up to their table and asks, "What are you having, hun? Can I get you something to drink?"

"We don't have menus yet," Robert says, smiling. "I was waiting for my friend."

The waitress steps away, returning with menus and a glass of water for Carly. "I'll give you a couple minutes."

Carly turns her attention back to Robert as the waitress walks away. "Okay, so we were close?"

"Well, we got together for fun and sex, some kinky, wild, totally uninhibited sex. And did I mention fun? I never met anyone like you before. You said the same about me."

"Kinky sex? What kind of kinky sex?"

Robert takes a deep breath. "Well, you rock my world. I've really missed you."

"Would you tie me up and beat me or hurt me?"

"I'd *never* hurt you. Yes, I'd tie you up or handcuff you and other things, but there's more to it. There was never…it's complicated. You don't remember anything?" Robert pauses, taking in an abated breath. "There's a balance of pain and pleasure that makes sex more…um…well…it's kind of advanced sexuality, but nothing that would harm you or me in any way. I'd *never* hurt you or do anything you didn't want me to do."

The waitress approaches again. "Are you two ready to order?"

Carly sighs. *A welcome interruption.*

Robert orders first. "I'll have the Big Bacon Burger plate with fries and a Hefeweizen."

"And you, dear?" the waitress asks.

"I'll have the Cobb salad with the house dressing on the side. Water is fine, thanks."

After the waitress leaves, Robert continues. "We experimented with sex. We discovered together that sometimes things we thought would be great, because it appeared that way in a movie, when we tried it in real life, the reality didn't live up to our expectations. The kind of sex we had, it increased our senses and adrenaline and pleasure. I'm not sure of the science, but it has something do with hormones. A lot of what makes sex magical occurs in our mind."

Robert pauses and shakes his head, motioning to her arm. "You don't think I did this to you? I would never!"

"How often did we see each other? Did we only get together for sex, or were we closer or more casual friends as well?"

"We'd go out to a movie once in a while. Sometimes, we'd go to museums, sketch and take notes. We'd go on art field trips. We once took a trip to Puerto Vallarta, and many, many times we went out to dinner. You've even came along as my significant other more than a few times to work parties."

"Would you describe a typical night we'd get together? It might help jog my memory."

"I'd rather show you."

"I don't think I'm ready for anything too serious." Carly raises her broken arm. "I'm winged."

"Well, I see your point, but a familiar location–familiar music, food, smells, sounds, *feelings*–they could help your memory return. I do want you to remember me–to remember us."

"Well, that's why I'm here." Carly considers that Robert may be right. It might help. "Okay," she concedes. "But not today."

"Your turn. What happened? Do you have any idea how you ended up like that? What happened to you?"

"Here's your beer, sir." The waitress places the frosted glass on a small napkin in front of Robert and leaves.

"Not much to tell, really," Carly continues after a moment. "Some guys found me beaten up in a 7-Eleven parking lot. My arm had what they referred to as a greenstick fracture and three of my ribs were badly bruised. I must have hit my head pretty hard 'cause I was unconscious for a while. They told me I had a concussion. I had to get a ton of stitches. I lost a lot of blood. I'd been tied up or handcuffed, and that was a few weeks ago. When I woke up my memory was gone. I didn't know who I was, or how I got in that parking lot, or how I got hurt." Carly, suddenly overwhelmed with emotion, bows her head, trembling. "Maybe we need to change the subject."

Robert puts an arm around her. "It's okay."

Robert's touch sends another torrent of physical sensations and emotion through Carly. Her vision narrows and begins to go black. "I think I need to go home. I feel like I'm gonna faint."

"Okay, come on. Let's get you home." Robert waves to the waitress. "Can we get the food to go?"

The waitress returns with bags of food and the check, which Robert signs and leaves on the table. He picks up the bags, then helps Carly out of the booth. "What's your address?"

"You don't know where I live?"

"We always went out or were over at my place. You never let me into your place before."

"Ah...let me see. I'm not sure I remember." She looks at her driver's license. "1452 West 18th Street, apartment 303."

Robert helps Carly into his car, an older black Honda Accord. "I know where that is. We're not far away."

As they reach her apartment building, Robert says, "Just a minute, let me help you up to your apartment."

"I'll be okay." Carly tries to get out of the car on her own but stumbles. She groans, her ribs ache.

"Always so independent. That's one of your charms, but right now you're not as okay as you think. I'm helping you up there." Robert puts an arm around Carly and supports her weight as they make their way to her apartment.

His insistence causes her anxiety to skyrocket, her stress heightened by the small elevator. She leans on the railing affixed to the wall as Robert lets go of her.

Carly breathes a sigh of relief when the chime dings and the doors open. She steps into the hallway, putting her arm around Robert once again for support, the movement of the elevator turned her stomach. "I really need to be careful mixing my meds."

"Where are your keys?"

Carly digs into her purse and hands the keys to Robert. He unlocks the door, flashing Carly a reassuring grin. They enter her apartment. Carly holds on to the edge of the door as firmly as her weakened hands will allow, her body somewhat blocking the entrance. "I need to lie down," she says, fighting to remain standing against a wave of dizziness threatening to drop her to the floor. "Thank you so much for helping me get home safely. You don't need to stay. I'm fine."

"Sure I can't stay and do some guard duty?"

"I'll be okay. I have the police on speed dial."

Robert leans in, wraps his arms around Carly, and gives her a nurturing kiss on the forehead. He inhales deeply. "I love the way you smell. Okay, be well, my lady. If you need anything, call me. We're like family–really–only better. There isn't anything I wouldn't do for you."

Carly feels the warmth of Robert's body and smells his muskiness with his arms around her, sending a rush of emotion through her, creating a yearning to see him again.

CHAPTER FOURTEEN

SECOND THERAPY APPOINTMENT

Carly gets out of the cab and walks into Dr. Mentes' office. *Lilacs. That's the smell.* She feels comforted by the new-found familiarity of this place.

A clipboard with Carly's name on a sheet of paper with a pen attached sits at the corner of the front reception area. Below Carly's name are instructions to fill out the attached questionnaire.

How are you sleeping?

Not sleeping, having nightmares, startling easily, jumpy and anxious.

How are you feeling?

Feeling numb, confused, sad and angry.

Any thoughts of suicide?

No, have only been trying to figure out what is going on and get my memory back.

Do you feel anyone is trying to hurt you?

Do I? Do I feel anyone is trying to hurt me? What if I know someone is. Does that count?

After Carly responds to the questionnaire, she rings the desk bell and takes a seat.

After a few minutes, Dr. Mentes appears with a young woman who had been crying. Dr. Mentes states,

"Okay, I'll see you next week, same time." The young woman nods and departs.

"Hi, Carly. I'll be right with you. Please go in and have a seat, anywhere you like."

Carly nods and smiles and walks back to Dr. Mentes' office. She once again settles into the same comfy chair she sat in the last time, with her back to the wall where she can see the door. *Why am I so anxious*?

Dr. Mentes enters shortly after. She glances down at the weekly depression paperwork and asks, "How are you doing? Have any memories returned? Anything new come up?"

"Well, I'm really upset. I've been getting harassing phone calls. On top of that, I went to the police station the other day. One of the officers who works in homicide told me they think the guy who beat me up is a serial killer, and somehow I got away."

Shaking her head, Dr. Mentes states with widened eyes, "What?! I'm probably understating this, but no wonder you're feeling upset!"

Carly nodding states, "I'm jumpy and haven't been sleeping well and startle at the slightest thing. I had the feeling someone was following me. Now I learn someone *is* possibly trying to kill me.

"Also, I was looking at pictures in my room and didn't feel anything. I was just numb. I don't have any memories of the man and the child in the photos. Do you know who they are?" Carly holds up one of the photos.

"I believe those are pictures of you with your husband and daughter."

Sadly, Carly lowers her head. "I can't remember my daughter or my husband?"

"You have a lot of stressors in your life right now. You are recovering from injuries. Someone is calling you and leaving you threatening messages. The police tell you a serial killer may be after you. And on top of all this your memories are mostly gone. What you are feeling is completely normal considering all the circumstances."

"Normal?" Carly repeats somewhat sarcastically.

"At the very least, expected."

"Last night, I had another nightmare of people chasing me, trying to kill me. I woke up, scared to death. From what I read in your therapy session notes, this isn't a new thing."

"Nightmares, especially ones that evoke strong emotions, can be very unsettling," Dr. Mentes states in a sympathetic tone. "What was the bad dream about? Did you have any new feelings or memories return related to the nightmare?

"No. Yes. Well, maybe. Do you know what happened to my daughter and husband? Why aren't they around?"

"Well, I didn't want to give you this information too soon. Carly, I'm sorry to say they're both deceased."

Shocked, Carly yelps. "What?! They're *both dead*? Do you know what happened?" A lump forms in the back of her throat, choking her. "Are you sure?"

Faltering, Dr. Mentes states, "The police aren't sure about all the details. They died a year or two ago."

Shaking her head, Carly presses further, "Did they die in a car accident? Were they murdered?"

Dr. Mentes counsels, "I'm not sure it's wise to visit this right now, given how you're feeling. Today, I would like to focus on how you're feeling now, about current events."

"Well, I'm sad, and now I'm angry too. Why didn't you tell me?" As her rage rises, Carly covers her face with her hands, wiping away hot, stinging tears. "Why didn't you tell me?"

Dr. Mentes sighs. "I understand how you feel. Do you remember what I said about transferring your feelings from something going on in your life onto me?"

Carly shakes her head. "I don't remember." Her anger continues its upward trajectory.

"This is a natural occurrence that sometimes happens in therapy. I'm a neutral party who cares about your well-being. I hope you can see you're angry at the circumstances in your life and are directing them onto me. I understand this is all confusing and sad and extremely frustrating."

Carly, agitated, shakes her bowed head. "Okay, I understand what you are saying, but I'm still really upset."

"There have been some horrible things that have happened to you, but I'm on your side. I have told you and am telling you what I think you need to hear, what you're ready to hear. Let's try to focus on other things in your life for now. Let the other information unfold gradually, so it doesn't overwhelm you. I've chosen to do what I think is in your best interest."

Maybe she's right. I do kinda feel like I'm drowning in a morass of maddening confusion. I just don't know why. Nodding, Carly heeds her counsel. "I went to see an old friend. About the closest I got to any memories was a familiar feeling."

Dr. Mentes smiles. "Good. Do you think he is a close friend?"

"He said we were close. I don't remember. I did have a strong physical reaction to him. I felt totally lit up. He turned me on. When he touched me, I felt lightning surging through my body, and I almost fainted. I dunno, maybe it was pain meds, maybe it was because I'm still recovering from injuries."

"Some good feelings are surfacing. I'm glad to hear that." Dr. Mentes smiles.

"The other night when I couldn't sleep, I was reading over your therapy session notes and have a ton of questions about what we were talking about, about my childhood. I read part of your diagnosis as schizoid issues. What exactly is that?"

"Well, it is somewhat of a broad category. For you specifically, you have difficulty connecting with people. You end up going through the motions of what appears to be connecting, but you struggle to feel it emotionally."

Hearing this, with eyes downcast, Carly sadly shakes her head. "Also, I read that you assessed me as having dysthymia–that means depression, right?"

"Yes, well, dysthymia is a diagnosis of long-standing depression. You were coming to see me at first for having a lot of anger and that you didn't know why you were so angry and didn't feel connected to anyone. The more we talked, the more we uncovered. I learned you were very depressed and had been for a long time. Outwardly, you'd been going about your life and acting nice, but underneath you had a great deal of buried, seething anger."

With growing sadness, Carly listens intently, with her head bowed.

"In my experience, anger is almost always a secondary emotion. You were very sad and most likely fearful and had never been able to express that. That sadness and fear and anger became intertwined and buried. I'm pretty sure you weren't even aware of the anger. You were angry, and rather than expressing that outwardly, you turned it inward, resulting in a deep depression."

"Did we find out why was I depressed?"

"The answer to that is a somewhat complex issue. It wasn't just one thing about your life causing this."

"Was my husband cheating on me? Abusing me? Was he an alcoholic or drug addict or something? Was I unhappy in my marriage, my work?"

Dr. Mentes smiles, takes a big breath. "Like I said, the answer is complex. You appeared to be very angry about being abused as a child, even though you weren't initially aware of it when our therapy started."

Abused as a child. The words reverberate in her mind and assault her senses. Carly takes in a deep breath.

Dr. Mentes continues. "We were working on you dealing with those feelings. You had repressed the memories. Other than sadness and sometimes momentary explosive anger that you almost always regretted, you had trouble feeling anything when I first met you."

Carly shakes her bowed head.

"I don't believe your husband had any of those problems you mentioned, although I do think he'd been drinking, but I don't think it was *the* problem. I believe your marriage became troubled and had to change because of what you were trying to deal with. This resulted in a strain between you and your husband. You were confronting your past and changing how you interacted with the world. Prior to our work, in my opinion, you were completely shut down emotionally."

"So, I was depressed and angry about my childhood?"

"Yes, but I was helping you come to terms with the abuse. I have done a lot of work with clients with repressed memories of being abused as children, notwithstanding popular belief that that there is no such thing as repressed memories. Right now, your past, and what is coming up for you is getting mixed up with and being complicated by your current memory loss. Please be patient with and kind to yourself. I was thinking, to help you through all this right now, would you consider taking an antidepressant?"

"I don't really like drugs of any sort."

"Well, these aren't drugs, *per se*. This would just be to help you get through a rough patch. I offered these to you once prior. I thought you could take something like Prozac or another SSRI. I also want to give you a prescription for Xanax, just in case you get super stressed. The Xanax is just meant as a stop gap in case you become so stressed that you're overwhelmed with anxiety. I want you to try to relax and heal up. Let your memories return to you when they're ready."

"How precisely do the SSRIs work? I don't want anything that interferes with my feelings or my thinking. And what does Xanax do?"

"The Xanax is what I want you use temporarily, just to relieve peaks in stress.

"The branch of drugs called SSRIs, very simply, make your brain retain serotonin, which is a hormone that helps you feel content. This doesn't cover up anything or make you feel drugged. It works gradually, and we'd start you on a small dose. Also, I have some more of our session notes for you. As you remember more, the more I think you'll be able to handle. When you're feeling up to it, after you've rested. Not today."

Carly takes the notes and the prescriptions from Dr. Mentes, overwhelmed and confused but with guarded hope.

"When do you want to come in again? How about Friday, 3:00?"

"Okay, thank you."

Carly steps outside the office, her mind a blur. She glances up and down and across the street, her gaze lingering on each passing person longer than usual. She shakes it off. *Was I always this paranoid?*

Overwhelming sadness and increasing frustration consume her with thoughts of her daughter and husband, as if their essence is somehow diminished by the mere fact that she cannot remember them.

An uneasy disquiet jabs at her. *Therapy is just making me feel worse.*

CHAPTER FIFTEEN

ANOTHER THREATENING PHONE CALL

Carly is awakened once again by an early morning phone call. She drifts back to sleep. The caller rings again.

The machine can pick it up.

The same unknown male voice, dripping with menace, whispers, “I’m watching you. Are you scared yet?”

Anxiety rises in Carly and her stomach tightens as she considers the message.

Is this that Tailor guy? *Does he know where I live? I probably need to tell the detectives about this.*

CHAPTER SIXTEEN

RESTLESS

Carly turns on her TV, mindlessly clicks through channels, hoping a distraction might calm her down. While the computer boots up, she strolls to the refrigerator, then back to the living room, stopping, glancing down the hallway. *Maybe some painting.*

Pacing around like a caged animal, Carly feels anxious, sad, and lost. *What is going on with me*? She kicks off her shoes, puts on *Kinda Blue,* goes to the kitchen, and pours a shot of Cuervo Blanco. She cuts a lime and rubs it on her wrist, then sprinkles it with salt. She drinks the shot, licks her wrist, and sucks the lime. She does that a second time, then a third.

She strolls down the hall to the second bedroom that functions as her studio, glancing through some of the ideas she has for paintings. She selects a picture of a woman sitting in front of a window on a rainy day. *This fits.* She sits down in front of a blank canvas and brushes on the first coat of color, a warm sienna. As the paint coats the canvas, accomplishment momentarily shrouds her anxiety.

While that dries, I'll read some more session notes. She sits down and opens her copy of the session notes.

May 14, 1997: Patient, Carly McCulley–
Continuing Diagnosis–PTSD, dysthymia, schizoid issues, insomnia, nightmares.
Rx: Continuing hypnosis.
Verbatim transcription of this date's therapy session follows:

Dr. Mentes: How are you today?

Carly: Something kind of strange happened. I was out walking, and I saw a child being taken back to her apartment by her father. The father was carrying her, and she was doing everything she could to get away and was crying bloody murder. "No, please don't, I don't want to go."

Dr. Mentes: Was he hurting her?

Carly: No, he was just carrying her in the opposite direction of the rest of the family. The whole family had passed me going one way, and then when I came around the block, the father was carrying this little girl back to their apartment. I became very anxious, and this situation caused me to get terribly sad. I started crying, like uncontrollable sobbing. I had to hold my right hand very close to me, as if protecting it, and I cried myself to sleep.

Dr. Mentes: What is the first thing you think about when you think of this girl? Was she in danger? What was happening to her?

Carly: I'm not sure. It felt as if my hand had been smashed.

As she reads this, a deep sadness descends on Carly like an untimely darkness before a thunderstorm.

Dr. Mentes: That was probably a body memory. Remembering something like this allows you to discharge a lot of negative emotion. I always liken pent-up emotions to shaking a bottle of pop. The pressure builds on the inside until the cap is taken off, then the pressure gushes out. While it isn't a happy event, it is healing. Have you had any more nightmares?
Carly: Well, the nightmare I was having that people were chasing me, trying to kill me, seems to get more and more specific until it was just one person. When I tried to focus on the dream, I had a memory flash. Like my mind opened up for a short time before slamming shut. I saw a young, blond-haired boy leaning over me massaging my private parts. At the same time, I was being held down by three or maybe four other boys.

Ire spikes inside Carly, assaulting her senses anew as she reads.

Dr. Mentes: How did that make you feel?
Carly: Really frightened. I was trying to figure out who the young boy was. I asked my brother if he knew of anyone who would have had access to me when I was younger. After repeated questioning and

much cajoling, he finally told me it was him and some friends. He was showing them how to have sex.
Dr. Mentes: How old were you, and how old was he?
Carly: I was about two or three, he was 13 or 14.
Dr. Mentes: He was showing them how to have sex? Did he say how, exactly?
Carly: No. In the memory flash, he was rubbing me around my vagina, and the boys were holding me down, and then everything went black…I was really scared, beyond reason. I lost my breath and felt like someone was trying to kill me. Maybe like someone was holding a pillow or something over my face. I don't remember any more. In hindsight, I think maybe he climbed on top of me, and I couldn't see anything because he was on top of me.

Anger quickly rises to rage, erupting inside Carly like a volcano.

Dr. Mentes: How were you feeling while talking to him about this?
Carly: At first, when I was talking to him, I was very angry and shaking deep inside. I had trouble keeping my thoughts straight. The more I talked to him I started to rage inside. I was really fucking angry, but I didn't want to share that I was angry because I wanted more

information from him. I don't usually share how I really feel with anyone.

Dr. Mentes: Did he say anything else?

Carly: I asked him if I looked scared. He said no.

Dr. Mentes: Did he apologize or say he was sorry?

Carly: No. He only said he didn't have any feelings toward me. Like, what the fuck was that supposed to mean? Maybe he only did it that one time. I asked him the names of the other boys. I actually contacted a couple of them. I was hoping they'd give me information to help me uncover my past. How naive of me, thinking that anyone would be honest about something that could potentially get them in trouble.

Dr. Mentes: Did he say anything else to you?

Carly: No!

Bastard. Stupid fucking bastard!!! Rage boils up inside Carly, smothering her senses.

Dr. Mentes: Is there anyone else you remember molesting you?

Carly: Is that what this was? Being molested? Why doesn't this seem like that to me?

Dr. Mentes: Well, when you grow up as part of a system, you kind of don't question anything. Events like this just become normal to you.

Carly: But it didn't seem like that.
Dr. Mentes: That was being molested. As a little girl you had a right to be protected and you weren't. I know that some of this is difficult for you to talk about, but I want you to try to remember any other incidents, with anyone.

A deluge of sadness drowns her rage, as Carly considers these words. *This is seriously messed up.* The reality of this information crushes Carly's mind.

Carly: Um…okay.
Dr. Mentes: Please know this is not your fault. I'm not making any judgments. You have many symptoms of being molested and of repressing those memories, but I did not want to diagnose without more information. Also, I wanted to avoid leading you to any false conclusions or memories.
Dr. Mentes: I want to give you a homework assignment. Go home, and think about times that something like this happened. Write down everything you can think of. Next time you come in, we'll discuss these.
Carly: Okay.

Carly contemplates what she just read trying to let it sink in. She feels deep anger and a palpable disgust in the pit of her stomach as if a snake is mercilessly tightening around her body. *This is horrible. No wonder*

I don't remember this stuff. Who would want to? She wraps her arms around herself and sighs. *Enough reading for today.*

Carly stands, strolls back to the kitchen, and has another shot of tequila.

CHAPTER SEVENTEEN

NEXT DAY

Returning from the doctor's office, Carly glances up and down the hallway outside her building's elevator. No one's there. After the phone messages, she's not taking any chances.

She darts down and across the hall to her front door. With nervous energy, she jiggles the key into the lock, rushes inside, slams the door behind her and locks it. She moves from room to room, hoping to find her place empty. When she does, she crashes onto the sofa and scratches her arm where her doctor just removed her cast. Her arm looks straight, but her pale skin, intermixed with a crusty, brown residue, appears sickly and smells awful.

Two more weeks away from work. I'm gonna go crazy. After fixing herself a tuna sandwich, she sits down to read some more of the transcribed therapy session notes Dr. Mentes gave her.

> May 21, 1997: Patient, Carly McCulley–
> Continuing Diagnosis–PTSD, dysthymia,
> schizoid issues, insomnia, nightmares.

Verbatim transcription of this date's therapy session follows:
Dr. Mentes: How are you feeling today?
Carly: I've been quite upset. I wrote down all the times I remembered something like what we discussed last time, of being molested or something like that. I remember feeling spacey when I was writing these down, and I've been angry and sad and obsessive. I just wanted to sit and stare out the window. I don't feel real. I keep running over in my mind how I must have caused this. Then I get angry and sad again. I feel like I want to break something or a lot of things.

Angry and sad *again*, Carly hangs her head and sighs.

Dr. Mentes: I believe a lot of the symptoms you're describing are a result of post-traumatic stress disorder, sometimes referred to as PTSD.
Carly: Like soldiers get after being in a war?
Dr. Mentes: Yes. But anyone can have PTSD when faced with life-threatening situations in which they had to shut down their emotions in order to survive.
Carly: So, you think someone threatened my life?
Dr. Mentes: Well, not in the way that soldiers face death. But when things happened to you at such an early age; what you described sounded as though you

were fearful and terrified with what your brother did. It seems the very people who should have been protecting you were hurting you. This is what the therapy process is, to get these events out in the open so your adult intellect can see what's happening and differentiate between those events in the past and what's happening in the present.
Would you like to share with me some of what you recalled?
Carly: Um, sure. In third grade I wore this pretty dress, and a boy who was in sixth grade sat across from me in the lunchroom. He shoved his foot up between my legs.

A sickened revulsion wells up inside Carly that makes her want to throw up. *I cannot believe this is my life.*

Dr. Mentes: How did that make you feel? Did the boy talk to you at all?
Carly: No. He just stared at me. I was really scared and felt sick to my stomach. I never wore that dress again.

Shame and sadness threaten to overtake the disgust and anger in equal measure. Even though she does not consciously remember this, she connects with it on a primal visceral level. Her stomach knots up.

Carly: After my mom died, my dad crawled in bed with me once and started caressing my belly and rubbing my nipples and running his hand in between my legs, and he said, "I know you want me."

Dr. Mentes: How old were you at the time?

Carly: About twelve or thirteen.

Dr. Mentes: How did that make you feel? Did anything else occur?

Carly: Really bad. I was stunned. I was actually asleep. At first, I just lay there paralyzed with fear. I was wearing a bra, a T-shirt, and another shirt over the top. I finally sat up and asked, "What are you doing?" He didn't say a word. He just got up and went back to his own bed.

Dr. Mentes: Do you have any other memories like this?

Carly: I have one more memory that I can think of. I was about five years old. I was sitting on the couch playing with my dad and hugging him and telling him I loved him, and I told him I was going to marry him. The next thing I knew, he had taken me back to his bedroom and was ramming his cock down my throat. He did that with such force it jerked my head backwards.

Even though she doesn't remember this, overwhelming rage darkens her mind. As fury wells up inside her, threatening to drown her, Carly takes a couple of deep breaths before continuing.

Dr. Mentes: I am so sorry this happened to you.

Carly: Describing this, I feel kind of spacey, like I'm disconnected from myself and floating.

Dr. Mentes: What you are describing is a form of dissociation called depersonalization. It is a defense mechanism.

Horrified, Carly is overcome with a confluence of suffocating rage, anxiety, disgust, and overwhelming sadness that clouds her thinking. *This just keeps getting worse. This can't be my life. I don't want to read any more of this*!

Carly puts on some Miles Davis and takes a Xanax. *I don't want to think about anything*. She sits on the window seat in her now favorite spot and stares out at the sky.

Who am I?

The phone rings. Carly lets the answering machine get it. "Carly, this is Robert."

Carly picks up the phone. "Hi," she says with a rush of giddy emotion.

"I was thinking we could go to dinner. What do you think?"

Carly hesitates. "I don't know. I just got my cast off, and I'm not really feeling up to doing anything."

"Oh, come on," says Robert in an upbeat tone. "Good food, great company, the perfect solution to what ails you. I'll pick you up at 5:30. How does that sound?"

"Well, okay."

"Awesome! See you then."

Carly ends the call and curls up in her seat. The surfacing emotions after reading those notes, eat away at her. The horrible stories battle with her desire to learn about her past.

CHAPTER EIGHTEEN

DATE WITH ROBERT

Carly waits for Robert in front of her apartment building. She fidgets, shifting her weight, glancing longer than normal at every car that drives past, at every person who walks by, wondering if they could be the creep who is stalking her.

Robert pulls up in his black Honda, gets out and comes around to the passenger side. “Hi, babe.” He leans down to kiss Carly’s hand. “It’s good to see you. How you feeling?”

Carly giggles. The touch of Robert’s lips on her hand overwhelms her with an explosion of feelings. Momentarily unable to speak, she smiles, then nervously says, “Okay, good.”

“I thought I’d take you to this little Mexican restaurant over on Vine. The Little Onion. They serve great margaritas and the best fajitas. They make their own tortillas. It’s a very cool place, family owned. Do you remember going there before?”

“No.”

“Well, you love their margaritas. Since you don’t remember, it’ll be a great new experience.”

Robert opens the car door. Carly slides in with excited anticipation.

As they walk into the restaurant, Carly notices a man dressed in classic gaucho garb: a brightly colored poncho draped over one shoulder, a black vest with matching pants, and a white, loosely tied scarf around his neck. He leisurely plays soft Flamenco guitar, while strolling around the restaurant.

A short, older woman in a multicolored, flowing dress, her hair neatly done up in a twist with a flower pinned at its apex, greets them and says in a beautiful accent, "*Buenos dias*, table for two?"

"Yes, please," Robert says with a pleasant smile.

They follow the woman to a booth. The table is covered with red linen, with white linen placemats, and a glowing, cylinder-shaped candle at its center.

"Here are your menus. Would you like anything to drink?"

"We'd like some margaritas, but we can wait for our server. It looks like you're swamped."

"*Gracias, señor*. Your server will be along shortly. Enjoy your meal."

Robert instructs Carly, "Look at the images on the walls around the room."

Carly glances at the bas relief mural painted in various hues of bright crimson, indigo blue, and warm sienna, extending around the dining area.

"Very cool, huh? It was painted to give the patrons the impression that they're in the midst of a bull-fighting ring."

"I see now. It's awesome."

"Part of why I brought you here was because you really like this place. I was hoping this might excite a memory. Also, this was the first place we went out to eat after we met."

Carly blushes. "I wish I remembered."

Robert smiles, though behind his grin Carly senses something more–sympathy, maybe frustration. Robert remains as much a mystery to her as the rest of her life since the assault.

She twitches her nose. "That aroma, what is it?"

"The tortillas."

"What was my favorite meal?"

"Not sure, but you always wanted to try new things. I remember you got something once that looked like a giant
spider, so you sent it back."

"Ewww, really? What was it?"

He shakes his head. "I don't remember."

A slight, dark-haired waitress approaches, smiling. "*Buenos dias, señor y señorita*, welcome back. The usual?"

Robert stares at Carly. She feels the pressure, as if she's on the spot. "Um, I don't remember...."

Robert interjects, "Golden Cadillac margarita, with an extra shot of Cazadores añejo on the side. Actually, make that two," he adds, smiling. "Also, we'll have a guacamole appetizer and a few more minutes with the menu."

"Very good, *señor*."

Robert scoots next to Carly and puts his arm around her. "Hey, you seem kinda nervous. Are you okay? It's all right you don't remember. Just try and relax and enjoy."

Carly takes a big breath and exhales. "I'll be fine. I just feel like...I'm a little keyed up. It seems like I have lots of stuff going on, even though I don't. I have nothing going on. It's boring the life out of me. Trying to remember and not knowing about myself makes me feel like I'm gonna explode or something. I feel...anxious and sad and frustrated and like I wanna crawl out of my skin," she says shaking her downturned head.

"Just breathe. I want you to relax. I won't move any faster than you're ready for, okay? We're friends first. I care about you. You're beautiful, and smart. You'll figure all this out."

Carly smiles. "Thank you for...well, letting me vent."

"Maybe it's your memories? Maybe they're trying to get out." Robert smiles right back.

"Could be." Carly exhales an exaggerated breath, while nodding in agreement.

The waitress returns with their margaritas. She places the drinks down on the napkins and douses each with a shot of Grand Marnier, placing the extra shot of Cazadores contained in the chilled, hourglass-shaped shot glasses next to their drinks. "Are you two ready to order?"

"Yes. You go first," Robert says, nodding to Carly.

"I'll have this," pointing to the menu item, "the 'Taste of Mexico' plate."

"Very good, and for you, *señor*?"

"I'll take the steak fajitas. Can I get some extra *tomalito* with that, please?"

"Of course. Is there anything else you'd like?"

"Not right now, thanks."

Carly licks her wrist, sprinkles some salt on it.

Robert grabs her arm and pulls it to his mouth. "Let me." He slowly licks the salt from her wrist while looking up at her. A shudder of exquisite energy courses through Carly, taking her breath away.

Carly smiles, feeling a little giddy. "What am I to do for salt now?"

"I'm sure you'll think of something."

Following his lead, Carly pulls Robert's arm over, licks his wrist and then sprinkles some salt on it, slowly licking it clean, mimicking Robert, staring at him the entire time.

They down their shots and smile. Robert takes a lime slice and places it up to Carly's lips, holding it there until she opens her mouth.

"I've missed you," Robert says.

Carly smiles. "Tell me again, what we used to do on a date?

"Well, like I said before, stuff just like this. We'd go out to eat, went to the movies, museums, painted together, went to concerts, or just hung out, and you'd cook for me, or I'd cook for you. One time, we drove to the

New York Metropolitan just to see a special *Degas* exhibit."

"And then?"

"Then we'd go back to my place and have some fun."

"Tell me more. Can you give me an example?"

"Like I said before, I'd really rather show you." As Robert says this, he reaches under the table and slides his hand up over Carly's leg, over her knee, and reaches up under her dress, and along her inner thigh. "You have panties on. You don't normally wear panties when we go out."

At Robert's touch, Carly is at first stunned but then experiences an intense rush of feelings, a mixture of embarrassment and intense arousal. Her loins throb. She holds her breath, trembling, momentarily losing her sense of reality. Attempting to speak, "I don't...I, really, um...what? Why, um...why not?"

"'Cause I asked you not to." Robert furtively glances around and, reaching Carly's sweet spot, starts to massage it.

Overwhelmed with self-consciousness and desire, Carly half-heartedly tries to push his hand away.

Undeterred, Robert continues the massage.

While she is drawn to this, wants it even, she also feels extreme discomfort. "Everyone's staring." She's sure they all know what's happening under the table, including the exquisite feelings spreading throughout her body from deep within. "I...I don't think I'm ready for this. I need some time."

Smiling, Robert whispers, "Try to relax."

Carly's breathing deepens. Shaking her head a little bit, she pleads, "Not here, please stop." Something about this just feels right–letting him take control of her. She feels vulnerable and exposed, yet at the same time bound to Robert in a powerful way, connecting with something primal, deep within her.

Robert moves his hand, allowing his fingers to linger, caressing Carly's leg. He lifts the back of his hand to his nose, breathing in deeply. He leans his head close to her ear, and with a big smile he whispers, "I love your smell. I love turning you on, letting you calm down, then doing that again, bringing you to the brink of pleasure. You rock my world, and I love to rock yours."

Carly's discomfort subsides, replaced by a calming warmth she's been longing for.

The waitress brings the guacamole and some chips and salsa and places them on the table. "Would you like another drink?"

"Not quite yet, thank you."

"Okay. Let me know if there's something else you need."

Robert states with a devilish smile, "There is something more I want, but *she* can't give it to me."

Carly giggles and sips the margarita. "I like these. This is exactly what I needed."

When the waitress brings their food, she asks, "Are you two ready for another drink yet?"

"Nah, we're good. In fact, we're great!"

Carly nods, smiling. "This smells amazing."

"Here." Robert picks up a sliver of steak and puts it up to Carly's lips. "Try some of this."

Carly takes it in her mouth, along with some of Robert's finger, which she allows to linger between her lips a moment before releasing it. She smiles up at Robert. The tequila warms and relaxes her. "I feel great. I haven't felt this wonderful since...I don't remember when."

"I'm pleased," Robert says with a big smile. "I kinda have mixed feelings about you not remembering any of this, or us, but at least I get to see you experience all this like it's the first time again. You know, people always ask if you could go back to any time and do something again, well, this would be it for me, getting to know you from the start."

"Yeah, but you know *all* about me. I don't know anything about you."

"Well, what do you wanna know? Ask me anything."

"Do you come from a big family? What kind of art do you do? What's your favorite food? What kind of music do you like? What's one of your best memories?"

"Whoa, slow down, let me think. I have two older brothers. My mom passed away a few years ago. Dad lives alone now on Long Island. What was the next question?"

"What kind of art do you do?"

"Well, I do motion graphics, storyboards, and action sequences for a big television network."

"Really? Which one?"

"CBS."

"Wow. You're a celebrity!"

"No, I'm just a regular guy. I snore and drink milk straight from the carton." Shaking his head, Robert sheepishly smiles and continues. "I like to draw and have dabbled in oils. I collect and like to hand-paint miniature cars. I'd really like to do more, but sometimes I work twenty days straight without a day off. What was the next...oh yeah, my favorite food is sushi. I love it. My favorite music is rock and roll or rhythm and blues."

"I think I like jazz, at least based on my music collection," Carly interjects.

"And my best time...my time with you has been my best time." Robert brightens as he recounts this memory. "There was one particular evening, we'd just started seeing each other, it was kinda like this, and we went out for dinner and drinks, danced, and went back to my place. We just connected."

Even though Carly connects to Robert's musings somewhere deep inside, sadly nothing registers in her conscious memory.

Robert enthusiastically continues. "We had such intense energy, I felt like the room was on fire. We couldn't get enough of each other. We came up for water and food about three days later." Robert laughs. "Maybe I could explain this in more detail, but I'd rather show you." Robert leans over, caressing Carly's hair, inhaling deeply. "I love the way you smell."

Carly's body surges with excitement, her stomach aflutter. She sips her margarita, finding her throat dry at the thought of Robert running his hands over her body, a thought that after the attack had seemed repugnant. She eases into the notion the physical contact might spark her mind, bringing more than just the sensation of touch but of memory as well.

After dinner, Robert takes Carly's hand and leads her out toward the parking area. As they reach his car, he pushes her up against the car door and puts his hand behind her head, running his fingers through her hair. He tilts her head to one side, almost kissing her neck, and inhales. He then whispers, "I want you. I want to be deep inside you."

Electrified, Carly feels weak with desire, her knees begin to buckle. For a moment, she loses her sense of space and time. "I, um...."

"You okay?" he asks with an impish smile.

"Yes, I just feel a bit weak. Not sure if it's the alcohol or the Xanax."

"Oh, dang, I didn't even think about you being on meds. Okay, I'll slow it down. I don't want you fainting on me. Let's go back to my place." Robert opens the door and helps Carly inside. He even helps her buckle her seat belt. "In you go. Don't want you running away. I've got you."

Carly breathes in deeply trying to calm herself. "I'm okay. I'm doing great, actually," she says with a big smile.

***

In short order, they reach Robert's apartment that sits atop a refurbished, multistory brick building in a somewhat rundown business area close to downtown, once home to warehouses and factories that have been reclaimed over the years. Creative graffiti adorns the fences along an empty lot adjacent to Robert's building, shielding views of cranes and structural steel rising up in what will soon be the latest neighborhood gentrification.

Excited, Carly enters an unassuming black door and looks around. "Wow, this is impressive." The sharp aroma of oil paint, Turpenoid, and freshly polished wood, tinged with men's cologne, infuses the space. Dark wooden floors and floor-to-ceiling windows grace the expansive loft. Interspersed on the walls are paintings of nudes in provocative poses, various drawings of knights and dragons, and an imposing carved stonework dragon dominates the center of the living room. Next to that on a plain wooden stand sits a statue of a man and woman in a passionate embrace. An easel stands in one corner, with long rectangular tables flanking it on either side, holding several palettes smeared with dried paints, as well as dozens of brushes bunched up in old fruit jars. A tilted drawing board occupies the opposite corner, sitting next to a large faux oak desk with three computer screens. Next to this lies a series of bulletin boards with numerous storyboards affixed, outlining the draft of some sequence of events in a sports arena.

"You have some gorgeous pieces here. Did you do this?" Carly asks, pointing at the stone statue that looks like a man and a woman half sitting, embracing and kissing.

"No, but I love it. It's *after* Rodin's *The Kiss*. Would you like another shot of tequila?"

"Sure!"

"All right. I got these special shot glasses. You told me once that you started drinking tequila when you saw the movie *Working Girl* with Melanie Griffith. Do you remember that movie?"

Carly shakes her head.

"Well, there's one line when Melanie's character is doing shots with Harrison Ford's character. She makes a statement that she had a brain for business and a bod for sin. You once told me you had a bod for sin. Maybe we'll have to watch that." He pours two shots of tequila and walks over to his CD player. He queues up "Iris" from the Goo Dolls' *Dizzy Up the Girl*. "This is one of my favorites," he says.

Carly pulls a lime out of a wire basket on the corner of the kitchen countertop and a knife off a magnetic holder affixed to the backsplash above the stove. She cuts the citrus into eight equal slivers. The knife handle feels smooth, the blade cuts straight and precise. *Well, I still know how to use a knife.* She looks for the salt. "Where do you keep the…." She opens one of the cupboards and finds it, then puts it on the table.

"This is good, you knew where the salt was," Robert says, smiling. "Let's see if we can bring up some more memories, but only the good ones."

"Are there bad ones?" Carly queries, tilting her head sideways and raising her eyebrows.

Robert walks over, wraps his arms around Carly, and dances with her, moving with the relaxed beat. "We'll move as slow as you need." Robert half-sings along, *"I just want you to know who I am."*

The closeness of Robert's body, the muskiness of his skin, the touch of his fingers on her back and neck, his hands around her waist, overwhelm Carly. "Am I floating?" Time slows to a standstill.

Robert smiles.

They sway back and forth for a long time.

"How are you feeling?"

"Um…good. Warm, safe."

"Awesome. I want to draw you. Whadaya think?"

Carly, enveloped in pleasure, stammers, "Hmm…wha-what?"

"I want to draw you. It'll give you a chance to relax."

"Okay, but…." She looks at her crusty brown arm fresh out of its cast, and thinks of her scars from the stitches and the legacy of bruises that have gone a pale, unattractive yellow ocher. "I'm still healing, what about…."

"Trust me. I will draw the beauty I see." Robert walks over to one of his tables and picks up a large drawing pad and a few charcoal pencils. "Take off your clothes."

"What?"

"Take your clothes off."

Stunned, Carly stands there blinking for a moment.

"I want to draw a picture of you–naked, just like Jack drew a picture of Rose in *Titanic*. It's just like going to the doctor, but we know each other." Robert smiles. "In the biblical sense."

Electrified and transfixed, she desires to please.

"Come over here."

Carly complies.

"Let me help you."

As Carly approaches, every cell in her body feels alive.

"Turn around." Robert undoes the back of her dress and pulls it down, running his fingers over her shoulders, then teasing her breasts, lingering down her sides and stomach, finally reaching her hips and legs. Her dress slips loose, crumpling into a pile on the floor. Robert reaches down and picks it up and lays it on the back of a nearby chair.

"Don't move." Robert undoes her bra. As he pulls it off, he wraps his arms around her, cupping her breasts, massaging her nipples, kissing the back of her neck. "You are absolutely breathtaking."

Carly lowers her panties, then folds and places them on the same chair her dress is laying on.

The heat from Robert's hands, the feel of his breath against her neck, electrifies Carly. She blushes. Closing her eyes, she weakens at his touch. Her desire intensifies. Her heart beats fast enough to trouble her breathing. These feelings overtake any reason from deep inside through her loins, gripping her with overwhelming lust that extends from her head down to her toes.

"Okay, lie down here."

Carly is momentarily drawn out of the euphoria.

Robert leads her by the hand over to the daybed and arranges the pillows. "Come."

With each step, Carly's heartbeat hastens. The blood leaves her head, threatening to cause her to faint. As she lies down, Robert caresses her and kisses her as he poses her, increasing the intensity of her arousal.

Robert retrieves a sheer piece of lavender lace from a far corner of his studio. He drapes it across her, allowing his fingers to glide over her skin as he displays glimpses of her body. He backs away a short distance to survey his creation, returning twice more to rearrange the lace. Each time, he continues caressing her and inhaling deeply as he moves closer to her neck, breasts and mound. "You okay?"

Carly's body burns bright red, as if she's about to explode. Her heart continues its excited throbbing in anticipation. Breathlessly, she responds, "Yeah…um…I'm good."

"Relax. It's just me." Robert runs his fingers across her cheek. "You're safe."

She breathes in deeply, settling back against the pillows, trying to calm herself even though she feels super energized, as if her body might ignite and explode at any second.

Robert lightly touches Carly's forehead with his index and middle fingers and begins to trace the contour of her body, starting up over her nose, lingering on her lips; then continuing down over her chin, around her neck, around the curve of her breast, up to a nipple, down the center of her abdomen, around her hip, across her mound, down the inside of her thigh, around her knees, down to her ankles, and finally her feet and toes. He glances up to lock eyes with her. "Try and lay still."

With mounting overwhelming excitement, Carly takes a deep breath. "What are...."

"It's my process." Cupping her cheek, he gently kisses her on her forehead then deeply kisses her lips, taking her lower lip into his mouth, momentarily sucking on it.

An intense bolt of energy pulses through Carly's body.

Robert turns off several lights, moving and adjusting his special diffuser light that casts perfect shadows over Carly's body. With the flick of a lighter, he sets several candles burning. "This makes for good art light. Much like having opposing forces of pain and pleasure, you need a sharp contrast of dark and light to create an alluring picture."

Sitting down with his drawing pad he begins to sketch. As Robert's eyes move over her body, erotic surges of exquisite energy pulse through Carly, caressing her with each stroke of his pencil.

Robert sprays the finished drawing with Fixatif, then carefully inserts it in a mat.

To see the finished picture, Carly walks up behind him, the lavender lace wrapped loosely below her shoulders, and partially draped to the floor. "This is stunning."

"It's the subject matter. I just drew what I saw." He takes Carly in his arms. "This is for you," he murmurs, kissing her deeply. "You are stunning. One of the best parts of my life."

While Carly is wrapped in his arms, she feels faint. "Whoa, I feel…." *Maybe too much tequila.* Carly's knees begin to buckle. Reaching up to caress his face, with a dreamy smile she says, "You are a beautiful man."

"Okay, I think this is enough excitement for one evening. Let's get you home."

For as nervous as she was when Robert had suggested they return to his loft after dinner, a twinge of disappointment strikes Carly's heart. The evening went better than she'd expected. Now, pondering what normalcy in a life all but forgotten might have looked like, she hopes that the ecstasy of tonight will continue.

CHAPTER NINETEEN

THIRD THREATENING CALL

Carly floats all the way to her apartment. *Why can't I feel like this all the time*?

Hand in hand, Robert and Carly slowly walk up to her door. "Good night, sweetness." He kisses Carly, wrapping his arms around her, lifting her off of her feet.

"I had the best time." Carly's face is sore from smiling so much.

"When you get better and all this is behind you, there will be much more of this, I promise. I'm not going anywhere."

He leans in and kisses her. The touch of his lips on her skin lingers after he turns and departs. Carly fights the urge to invite him upstairs. Hesitating, she says, "Good night."

Once inside her apartment, Carly looks around, still feeling as if she's floating, hoping the sensation isn't just her pain meds mixed with tequila.

I feel absolutely wonderful.

She presses the flashing light on her answering machine.

Heavy breathing churns from the speaker, setting Carly on edge.

"I'm watching you."

A surge of adrenaline shoots through her. Dread fills her mind, replacing the ecstasy of her perfect night.

I need to tell Detective Daugherty.

Carly's mind drifts back to Robert. *This is good. Finally, a bright spot.* She smiles thinking of his touch, thrilling her body from the tingling in her breasts down to the throbbing in her loins. Giggling with delight, she breathes in deeply, remembering the smell of his skin, the warmth of his body next to hers, and his gorgeous blue eyes. *I'm never going to get to sleep now.*

Carly crawls in bed and tries to fall sleep. She tries to focus on Robert, but the voice on the message ominously lingers in her mind.

CHAPTER TWENTY

IGNORING TRUTH NEVER CHANGES IT

Carly rolls around in bed for an hour, trying to fall asleep, mulling erotic thoughts of Robert, all the while battling intrusive anxiety over the voice message.

Robert is completely amazing. I'm not going to get to sleep anytime soon, so I might as well look at photos or read from Dr. Mentes' therapy session notes.

Hoping some jazz music will help relax her, Carly queues up *The Best of Sam Cooke.* She smiles as she listens to "Wonderful World."

Opening one of the leather-bound photo albums from the shelf, Carly cozies up in her favorite chair and flips through the pictures. After viewing dozens of pictures of a bright, smiling, adorable baby girl, sadness seeps into Carly's thoughts, leaving her forlorn and confused.

Why can't I remember her? I want to remember her. I want to remember Robert.

At the thought of Robert, waves of pleasurable energy flow through her, distracting her from the photos. Carly closes her eyes and breathes in. Images of Robert's body, his eyes, his smell temptingly caress her mind.

What if he's the one who did this to me? It can't be him? The only way to know for sure is to get my memory back.

Needing to drown out the jumble of feelings, she pours a shot of tequila, drinks it down, then a second, impatiently waiting for the euphoria, something, anything to numb herself out.

Maybe if I do some painting or drawing–I can get past whatever's holding my memories back. I'll draw what I don't want to see. That's served me well before, drawing and painting my feelings.

Taking out a sketch pad, Carly starts to draw but ends up mindlessly scribbling, then grinding the pencil into the paper. The pencil tip snaps. Fresh anger fills her to her core.

Hoping to distract herself, Carly opens the therapy notes once again. As she begins to read, a sense of trepidation descends over her like a dense stifling fog.

Excerpt from transcribed therapy session notes:
August 14, 1997: Patient, Carly McCulley – Continuing Diagnosis–PTSD, dysthymia, schizoid issues, insomnia, nightmares.
Verbatim transcription of this date's therapy session follows:
Dr. Mentes: How are you and your husband getting along?
Carly: Um, I dunno. I guess okay.
Dr. Mentes: Do you two ever argue or fight?

Carly: No. We're nice, very cordial to one another.
Dr. Mentes: Cordial? What happens when you disagree?
Carly: We don't. We're very nice to each other.
Dr. Mentes: Has anything changed recently?
Carly: I don't want to have sex with him anymore, not that I ever did, but up until recently when I started having these nightmares, I always felt something was wrong with me that I didn't understand, and I wanted my marriage to work. I always did what I thought was expected of me. I guess I had preconceived notions of marriage and kept thinking, if I was just good enough somehow, things would magically change.
Dr. Mentes: How does he feel about you not wanting to have sex? Do you talk about that?
Carly: No. And I don't initiate it. I don't say anything. Maybe this is part of my anger. I guess on some level I want to. I need to stop pretending.
Dr. Mentes: Did you ever enjoy sex with your husband?
Carly: No. I was never attracted to him, physically or emotionally. I did not understand all this.
Dr. Mentes: You married him, though. What brought you to make that decision? You must have liked him.

Carly is deeply saddened reading this. She aches for what never was because somewhere she passionately believed in her vows that included *until death do us part.*

Carly: Well, I guess it was a logical decision. I never really learned who I was and what I wanted or needed. He was smart and handsome and funny and had a good education and was kind and honest. He is a very good man.

***

August 30, 1997: Patient, Carly McCulley – Continuing Diagnosis–PTSD, dysthymia, schizoid issues, insomnia, nightmares. Verbatim transcription of this date's therapy session follows:
Dr. Mentes: How have you been since the last time I saw you? I know you canceled a couple of appointments.
Carly: Um, something really bad, um...awful happened.
Transcriptionist interjects: Sound of client crying for an extended period of time (more than 5 minutes).
Carly: My daughter was raped and murdered.
Dr. Mentes: Oh Carly, I'm so sorry.
Carly: Then a couple weeks later, my husband shot himself.

These words assault her anew, with the force of a freight train hitting her. *This is too much*! *I'm...I don't know what I am. I have to...I don't know....*

Carly stops reading, awash with a bewildering torrent of undifferentiated feelings. As her gut tightens with rage, that spreads throughout her body like unwelcome poison tendrils attacking a defenseless plant, she drops the therapy session notes and buries her face in her palms. Tears sting her eyes.

Angry, distressed and deeply saddened, Carly feels as though she was kicked in the stomach. She curls up in her favorite spot by the window and squeezes her knees to her chest. Shaking her down-turned head, her mind wanders. Unanswered questions race through her mind–*my daughter, my husband. How? Why? What happened?* After replaying those words over and over, too fatigued to struggle against the mix of anger and sadness that weakens her, overwhelming her senses, she drifts off to a fitful sleep.

CHAPTER TWENTY-ONE

ANOTHER DREAM

Vulnerable and frightened, Carly walks alone on an uneven path strewn with tree roots, enveloped by the earthy smell of the jungle throbbing with life. Every manner of animal sound and bird call invades her ears. Intense sunlight cuts the darkness of the canopy of trees above, piercing the openings between the branches.

Carly continues walking while gale-force, supercharged wind, like that engendered by a dangerous thunderstorm, pummels her body, caressing her, arousing her.

She arrives at a clearing and notices a tiger spying on her from behind bushes on the other side. Paralyzed with fear, she cannot move or run or breathe. Adrenaline-fueled terror pulses through her, continuing to rise, as she remains locked in a stare down with the big cat. Finally, the tiger moves toward her, its massive shoulders rising and falling with each step. It charges.

The tiger leaps directly at Carly's core, melding itself into her body. As it does, the panic she feels crescendos in waves until every cell in her body is electrified, consuming her with the most exquisite and intense energy surging through her, bringing her to a peak of emotion.

Carly bolts awake, sweating, breathless. She blinks, staring at her surroundings. *It was just a dream.*

CHAPTER TWENTY-TWO

BIG RED "S"

Daugherty sips his aromatic coffee, gazing through the blinds and out the window at a drab, gray morning. He hears Detective Franklin's ponderous cadence come from the elevator bay and enter the room. He turns to see Jim disappear behind the dividers that surround his desk.

Daugherty walks over to Jim's area. A sharp pang hits Daugherty's gut as he considers his question. "Hey, Jim."

Abruptly, the typing stops. "Hi. What's up?"

Daugherty hesitatingly asks, "Do you think there's any reason why I couldn't take Carly on a date?"

"What? The victim in our open investigation? Are you serious?"

"Well, she's not a person of interest. I just feel, um…I want to…um…I feel protective of her."

"Wow, I can just see the big red *S* on your chest. Do you have a cape too?"

"What?"

"You have a Superman thing going on. You know, you want to try to be a hero and protect Carly from the bad guys, or in this instance, *the* bad guy."

Detective Daugherty sheepishly smiles.

Cocking his head sideways, Jim asks, "You haven't been following her, have you?"

"I'm concerned about her," Daugherty protests. "I *want* to protect her. And *you* said to keep low-profile surveillance on her."

"*You–have!* You've been following her?" Jim shakes his head, raising his eyebrows. "That's not your job. Let the protective detail handle this."

"Even though your background check didn't show her friend Robert Hoy to be a potential perp, I just wanted to make sure he didn't try to hurt her."

"What do you mean you wanted to make sure *he* didn't hurt her? Have you been watching her with her boyfriend?"

Reluctantly, Daugherty nods his head.

"You perv! So, you tailed her while she was on a date? What happened?"

"Well, they went to eat at the Little Onion. Then they went back to his place. They did some shots of tequila. They laughed. They danced. He undressed her. He drew her. Then he kissed her good night and took her home."

"Damn! Listen to me. That's insane! Watching them when you have feelings for her. You're asking for trouble."

"Yeah, I know. I mean, he undressed her...and...drew her."

"Drew her, what?"

"He's an artist. He drew a picture of her. It was fascinating to watch." Daugherty sits picturing it again, enthralled.

"Why did you become a policeman?"

"My sister was attacked and raped by a stranger at 15. No one was there to help her. She was never the same after that. She ended up taking her own life at 22."

Jim shakes his head. "I'm sorry, man. Carly's story is kind of like that, isn't it? Do you think you're going to be able to protect her when you weren't able to protect your sister?"

"Um...maybe. I really hadn't thought of that before. I can't let the same thing happen to her. And I still have my job to do."

"Okay, so you claim to be following her because you want to, what, make up for not being there for your sister? Your sister? Yeah, right." Jim shakes his head dramatically, his voice filled with sarcasm. "Who exactly are you trying to convince? You have the hots for your vic. Admit it."

"It's a lot more than that! I like her. I *care* about her," Daugherty protests. "Come on, you know me."

"Face it. You are *not* following this lady around just because you want to make sure she's okay. You're jealous!"

"All right. Fine, maybe you're right. Okay, yeah, she turns me on. I tried to keep it business. I tried to distance myself, but I'm just drawn to her. That doesn't mean she doesn't need someone looking after her."

"You should wait until the case is over and we find out who the bad guy is."

"Yeah, but this case might never get solved. She might get killed in the process. I don't see the harm. She's not a suspect, and...I like her."

"Man, don't confuse your protective instinct with attraction. This may be some fucked-up duty thing you think you owe to the universe or something, and not romantic attraction at all. Maybe you're just attracted to duty, or honor, or being a hero."

Daugherty nods. "I hear ya."

Jim shakes his head and smiles. "I don't think this is the best idea you've ever had. Just saying, man. Think about this long and hard. I am *strongly* advising you to wait. Don't get too involved in this. It'll cloud your judgment if you do."

CHAPTER TWENTY-THREE

CALLBACK FROM COUSIN

"Carly? It's Sarah. I'm sorry I didn't get back to you sooner, but I was on vacation. My friend who took the message was dog sitting for me and didn't give me the message right away. How are you doing?"

"Hi, Sarah, thanks for calling back. I'm doing okay. Well, not exactly okay but mostly okay. A lot has happened recently."

"What's up?"

"I'd called because, um, well…." Carly hesitates, realizing she doesn't really know this person and doesn't know how she feels about sharing all the details of her life.

"You don't call that often. This must be important."

"Well, I'm okay, I guess, but I lost my memory. I was hoping maybe you could fill in some blanks for me."

"Lost your memory? How'd that happen?"

"I'm not sure. I woke up in the hospital. I got beaten up. A couple guys found me unconscious in a parking lot."

"What!"

"I know, it's kinda shocking."

"Kinda shocking! Seriously!"

"When I woke up, I couldn't remember who I was or what happened. I've gone to see my therapist a couple times, and a friend and a really nice police officer are helping me, but I'm still just kinda in the dark about...almost everything. I was hoping maybe you could tell me about my family, you know...about my mom and dad, my past, my husband and daughter."

"I'm so sorry, sweetie. I'd be glad to. And, um, that's a lot of ground to cover. What are some–"

"Were you and I close? How well did we know each other? I did have one memory return related to you. You were fixing my hair. You put some perfume on me. The same perfume I still use–White Shoulders."

"Yes, I remember that."

"Whatever you have time for and want to share with me I'd appreciate greatly."

"We lived next door to each other growing up. Our mothers were sisters. I'm a few years older than you. We'd play together sometimes. Grandma Tilley used to take us fishing and out to pick dandelions. I think she made wine out of those. You moved away when you were nine or so, and I haven't had a lot of contact with you since."

"Tell me something about yourself. Maybe we can, I don't know, reconnect."

"I'm a licensed clinical social worker for the North Carolina Health Department. I do assessments and therapy and travel around helping crisis victims. I'm married and have two children. What else can I tell you?"

"What do you know about my family–my husband and daughter? You knew my mom and dad, right?" Carly swallows hard. "And, this may not be easy to talk about, but was I abused as a child that you know of?"

"From what I remember your mom was a beautiful and talented woman." Sarah pauses. "She loved you very much. Your mom died when you were eleven from complications of multiple sclerosis. She had been sick for a long time prior to that, unable to walk for many years. You all moved away a year or two before she died, so I didn't see you much. Grandma Tilley had died a year before that. I got to fix your hair for her funeral."

"What about my dad?"

"Um, your dad, he was...he made the best bread. I can still remember the smell of it. But, your dad, Dave, was an angry, crippled man."

"Crippled?"

"Yeah, he walked with crutches the entire time I remember him. He had osteoarthritis. His hip joints had disintegrated. Both of your parents had really bad luck with their health. I believe your dad also drank a lot."

"So, was I abused as a child? Specifically, was I molested? Do you know?"

"Hun, I'm not sure I'm the best person to be reconnecting you with this part of your past like this."

"No, please, go on. Thank you for this. I'm hoping some of this information will trigger my memory, you know, to help it come back."

"I only remember hearing Mama and Grandma talking about a suspicion of theirs. Your dad slept in the same room with you, while your mom slept somewhere else, maybe on the couch. I think they thought that was kinda odd. I'm pretty sure Mama suspected it."

"Did anyone ever do or say anything?"

Sarah takes a deep breath. "Not that I'm aware. Incest is something most people are extremely uncomfortable discussing and really don't want to think about it, or know about it, let alone talk about it. It seems, generally in my practice, if they do know about it, they deny or ignore it. Talking about it and outing people is a whole 'nother level of difficult.

"Some people have a hard time just discussing regular feelings with one another, let alone subjects that make them really uncomfortable, especially subjects related to sex. Our society is repressed when it comes to sexuality. I think many people want to believe, or at least somewhere in their minds, hold to the belief or make-believe things are better than they really are. I think we humans are like that. Otherwise we'd just live in the constant pain of reality."

"Did you know my husband, my daughter?"

"Well, let's see. You married a man you met at your church. Honey, are you sure you want me to tell you what I know? What I think I know may not be the truth, just my impression of it."

"Yes, well, I read something about my husband and daughter, so I know they're dead."

"I'm so sorry. A couple years ago, or maybe last year, your daughter was found dead. Not too long after that, Ben–your husband–died. I don't know all of the details. It was a rough time for you. I tried to reach out, but it felt like you pushed me away." Sarah takes a deep breath, pausing before she continues. "You two had been having trouble, and you were in therapy trying to work on your marriage. Whenever we'd talk, you always wanted to talk about the past. The past is something I just want to move on from and let go of. I mean, you can't let things from the past control your present, or you'll end up missing your life."

Carly feels an awkward lump of emotion form in her throat.

After a moment, Sarah speaks again. "Most recently, I got the impression you were on a quest to find the person who had hurt your daughter. I thought that's why you took that job at the private investigator's office."

"Wow. Thank you. That's a lot. Do you remember anything else that might be important?"

"I remember that when you were very young, I'd see you and your dog running around. You were like a feral child, always dirty and barefoot. You had two parents who were old and infirm, and the last thing they were able to do was take care of a young child. This wasn't your fault. These were the circumstances you were born into."

"Again, thank you for sharing all this." Carly feels saddened at this new information.

"If you need to talk more, please call. I'm happy to help in any way I can. Maybe we can get together sometime. Let's try to stay more in touch, okay?"

"Sure. We'll have to get together soon."

"I live fifteen hundred miles away, but let's try."

"We will." Carly thinks Sarah is just being polite. "Thanks, Sarah. I really appreciate your help."

"Bye, Carly."

Carly hangs up and gazes toward the window, thankful for Sarah's call, for the information. She breathes in deeply, trying to relax, to let everything she'd heard sink in. A vague uneasiness descends upon her. She can't tell if her swirling thoughts and feelings are fresh reverberations from the conversation–or from the past. She grasps at phantoms, reaching for something new to materialize out of the haze of the past, something to tell her she's remembering. Every time she thinks she has something, it vanishes.

CHAPTER TWENTY-FOUR

A SECOND "NOT A DATE"

The phone rings. Carly hesitates. Her pulse quickens. She picks up the receiver. "Hello?"

"Hi, Carly. It's Detective Daugherty. I was calling to see how you've been feeling."

"I'm doing okay."

"I was wondering if we could get together so I could ask you some more questions. Have you had any memories come back?"

"Well, not exactly memories. I've read some notes from past therapy sessions, some really horrible things. I also had a chat with my cousin and learned a little about my past."

Daugherty asks in a hesitantly broken manner, "I was thinking I could talk to you…that we could...maybe over dinner or lunch? Sharing food will make this seem less like an uncomfortable chore. It's not a date, just part of my job."

Carly, smiling, says, "Sure, I guess. Sure."

"Okay, how's 12:30? When can you be ready? I'll come by and pick you up."

"I have a 2:30 appointment with Dr. Mentes today. How about after that, maybe for dinner?"

"What's your favorite type of food?"

"Italian."

"Excellent! That's a good sign, you remember your favorite food, or is this newly learned information? Have you ever been to Prego? Oh, wait, I'm guessing you wouldn't remember it. I really like their osso bucco."

He's really thoughtful. "I'll see you around 5 o'clock." Carly hangs up, feeling grateful for the kind attention and the distraction.

CHAPTER TWENTY-FIVE

THERAPY APPOINTMENT THREE

Now that she has her cast off, Carly decides to drive to her appointment. Even though her paranoia simmers, it remains in check, fading a little more with every venture out from her apartment. She looks for her car and warily approaches it, glancing over her shoulder, leery of anyone watching. It's a short trip. Carly parks in the lot next to Dr. Mentes' office. She breathes in deeply, enjoying the familiar scent of lilacs outside the building, comforted once more.

The clipboard with Carly's name on a sheet of paper with a pen attached greets her like an old friend. She reads and responds to the questions. *How are you sleeping? How are you feeling? Any thoughts of suicide? Do you feel anyone is trying to hurt you?* When finished she rings the bell and takes a seat.

After a few minutes, Dr. Mentes appears and says, "Hi, Carly, how are you doing? Please go in and have a seat. I'll be right with you."

Carly nods and smiles and walks down the hall to Dr. Mentes' office. She picks the same spot with her back to the wall where she can see the door, settling into the same comfy chair. *I wonder if I always feel this anxious coming in here.*

Dr. Mentes enters. “So, have any more of your memories returned? Anything new come up? Your call sounded like something happened.”

“Not new really, but I just read something in your therapy session notes about my husband and daughter that stunned me. I was really shocked when I read it. I guess, the truth hit home on some level, but I’m really upset about not remembering them or feeling anything about how they died. I’m just confused and feel like I’m drowning in darkness.”

Carly swallows hard. “How long was I coming to see you prior to my….” She struggles to even say it aloud, “my child’s and my husband’s deaths?”

Dr. Mentes kindly says, “Like I said before, you were coming to see me for a year or so prior to those tragic events. I’m not certain how long, but you were depressed and struggling in your marriage.”

“What are you not telling me?”

After pausing, Dr. Mentes says, “As I said before, I don’t want to just blurt out information until you’re ready to handle it. When you recently came in to see me with your arm in a cast and your bruised-up body, I didn’t think you were ready to receive a lot of this information. I’m not sure you’re ready to hear this now. I hoped your memories would return in short order, and I…we just need to trust the process that when you’re able, you’ll remember your life. You’re a strong woman, Carly, one of the most resilient people I’ve worked with.”

Carly nods.

"If you'd like, I could put you in a relaxed hypnotic state again. I think this may help you. At the very least it should help you bring down your stress level. Are you up for that?"

With trepidation, Carly says, "I trust you."

I think.

Dr. Mentes methodically leads Carly into the relaxed state. "Okay, sit back, and close your eyes. Try to relax, and just focus on your breathing." Dr. Mentes guides Carly through the now-familiar hypnosis process.

"Focus on your breathing. Walk up to the door at the end of the hall, open it, and step inside. When you do, I want you to envision a time when you were with your daughter and husband and you were happy."

"I'm afraid."

"I'm here with you. You can walk through there and just observe yourself with your daughter and your husband, as if you were watching a movie. You don't have to imagine actually being with them, you can just watch the events as if it's on a TV screen."

Carly nods. Filled with mounting anxiety, she reaches down and opens the door. Speechless, she stares, stunned at what she sees–the broken, lifeless body of her little girl lying on the floor, with her frilly, light-blue dress pushed up almost covering her face, her tiny panties ripped and dangling from one leg. Her legs and the area around her vulva are bruised and bloody. Her face is gray. Her lifeless, blue, tear-stained eyes are fixed and staring up at the ceiling. Carly gasps for breath.

Dr. Mentes asks, "What are you seeing?"

An excruciating lump grows in Carly's throat, choking off air, along with any emotion trying to escape. Carly bursts out sobbing and howls from her innermost depth. "No! Elizabeth!" *My baby girl*! *My beautiful baby girl*!

Shaking her head and covering her face, Carly cries with gut-wrenching, unabated sobbing for an uncomfortably long period of time. "I can't...believe someone," Carly's speech falters as she gasps for air, "that someone...would, could...do that to such a sweet...I need to stop. I need to go now." Carly's sadness becomes all-consuming rage–swallowing her. *How could someone have fucking done this*? *Goddamn them*!

"Carly, I want you to close the door and walk back up the stairs. As I count, see the doors–six, five, four, three. When you get close to the top of the stairs, you can...."

"Fuck your goddamn doors!" Carly yells, abruptly coming out of the hypnotized state.

"Carly, tell me what happened."

Carly screams with bottomless rage and sadness from a place so deep within herself, she feels as if she's suffocating in a quicksand-like mire of feelings, enveloping her, strangling her.

"I saw my...." Carly is overcome by uncontrollable weeping, and struggles to breathe as she chokes out, "My little, precious...daughter, how...could...someone?"

Dr. Mentes reaches over and lightly touches Carly on her shoulder, pushing a box of Kleenex on the coffee table closer to her reach, while Carly continues crying. Dr. Mentes sits there quietly.

From a place of deep darkness and despair, Carly says, "I feel as though my insides are shredding." She weeps again.

Dr. Mentes waits until Carly reaches a point where she isn't crying so deeply.

"What happened? What did you see?"

Carly takes a deep breath. "I'm not sure I can, or wanna, talk about this right now. I can't think about it."

"I can see this is very painful for you, as if you were experiencing it for the first time all over again. I want to help you process these feelings."

"Not now! I don't want to talk anymore. I can't! I don't want to. I need...I have to go!"

"Carly, I'm sorry this took you to that memory. I was hoping it would open a door to when you were happy. I'm sorry you're in so much pain."

Dr. Mentes pauses, allowing the silence between them to envelope and comfort Carly. "However painful this is, it means your memories are starting to surface."

Carly, consumed by grief, shaking her downturned head, sadly reflects, *I don't want to remember any of this. This is too much!*

***

By the time Carly gets home, a jumble of feelings–shock, confounded numbness, pain, and confusion threaten to consume her.

She steps inside her apartment, slams the door behind her, and bolts the lock. She slides down the door, her legs giving way. She holds her head in her hands and weeps.

After a while, she glances around. The light to her answering machine blinks an intermittent, ominous red.

Carly stands, walks to the answering machine and presses the button.

"I'm watching you. Don't you remember me or know who I am?"

Carly changes her friendly voice-message greeting to something pointed. "Hi, you've reached Carly. Please leave a message, unless you're the asshat creep who's been harassing me. Stop fucking calling!"

I need to tell Detective Daugherty about this.

Carly takes a Xanax and follows that with a shot of tequila. She walks to her CD player and puts on Natalie Merchant's "My Skin" from her *Ophelia* CD. She knocks back another shot of tequila, turns out the lights, and curls up in her safe spot by the bay window, staring out at the sky and the cityscape beneath it, sadly thinking back to the image of her daughter.

My sweet Elizabeth.

CHAPTER TWENTY-SIX

DETAILS

Upon hearing a firm knock on her door, Carly peers through the peephole and sees the distorted shape of Detective Daugherty holding something close to his chest.

She opens the door. Detective Daugherty offers her a single white gardenia. "Here, this is for you. This seemed a favorite fragrance of yours, and I thought it might cheer you up."

"You shouldn't have." Carly forces a smile. "I'm not quite ready yet. I've been draggin'. It's been a rough day. Come in."

Carly puts the flower into a small vase. The potent sweet floral scent of gardenia fills the room. "This is one of my favorites. Thank you for your kindness."

"I thought I smelled gardenias when I was in here before."

"That might be the perfume I use, White Shoulders."

"Well, I hope you like the flower. The scent is kind of strong though. Isn't it?"

"A little." Carly cocks her head, raises an eyebrow. "This is kinda date-type behavior, isn't it? I mean, flowers, dinner? Is this okay when I'm part of an ongoing investigation? I saw a movie once where the detective acted a lot like you. He turned out to be the perp."

Chuckling, Detective Daugherty says, "Perp? I had a similar conversation with one of my superiors. The officer you met previously. It turns out, we don't consider a victim a suspect, so this is perfectly fine. Like I said before, this isn't a date," Daugherty tries to clarify. "I just get to multitask. I can ask some questions to see if you remember anything, *and* I get to enjoy the company of a lovely lady over dinner. For me, that's a treat."

"You think I'm lovely?" Shaking her head. *This feels like dating behavior.*

"Well, I'm just trying to illustrate a point," Daugherty says, fumbling for words. "That's not the point. I wasn't trying to say that...I was trying to say that I'm glad you accepted my dinner invitation. Speaking of which, we'd better get going, the reservation is for 5:30."

Carly grabs her coat from a hook on the rack next to the door and follows Daugherty out of her apartment, not convinced that this isn't a date, for *him*.

Trying to change the subject, Daugherty asks, "How are you doing? I see you got your cast off."

"Yeah, finally. I just wonder when this will stop itching," she poses raising up her left arm. "Are there any more leads in my case? Has anyone found out what happened to me?"

"Not really. It's a difficult situation. Because of your memory loss, we don't know where your assault occurred. That makes it hard to develop any concrete leads."

Carly nods.

"You seem to be healing well. I'm glad."

It's a short distance to the restaurant. Daugherty parks at an open space a block down the street and quickly attempts to get over to open the door for Carly. She beats him to it, getting out on her own.

As they approach, Carly looks at the restaurant and the sign above the door boasting its name: Prego. "I don't remember this place," she says, somewhat apologetically, shaking her head.

"That's not a big surprise."

An expansive floor plan spreads out from the main foyer, its walls detailed in rich, paneled dark walnut. Pristine linen covers all the tables. The finery is offset by the open duct work, piping, and concrete blocks encompassing the space.

The hum of the dinner crowd blends with the smooth, relaxed music playing from the wall-mounted speakers. Many tables remain open.

Struck by a rising tide of uneasy emotion, Carly glances around at the clientele. She hadn't encountered so many people in one place, having avoided crowds or more than the few patrons on her date with Robert. The room is filled with an anxiety-provoking din of visual and auditory noise, coming from a mire of conversation and cellphones flitting on and off tabletops.

Carly focuses on the smells wafting from the kitchen. She closes her eyes and inhales, savoring the rich, welcoming aroma of garlic, basil, and warm bread, distracting her from the persistent and increasing anxiety welling up inside her.

A short, friendly looking woman with long, dark hair approaches them and asks. "Are you joining us for dinner? Is this for a special occasion?"

Detective Daugherty responds, holding up two fingers. "Yes. We have a 5:30 reservation under Daugherty, table for two. If possible, could you seat us somewhere quiet?"

"Follow me." She seats them away from the chatter of investments, briefs, and sales, in a far corner booth, laying menus in front of them.

Before leaving them, the hostess asks, "Would you like anything to drink?"

Both Detective Daugherty and Carly ask for water.

"Very good. I'll send your waitress over shortly. One of our specials today, which I'd recommend, is the arancini. Also, the roast duck is my favorite, and it comes with mixed-mushroom ragù and Grana Padano. Enjoy your dinner."

Another server brings them each a glass of water with a slice of lemon, places a basket of warm bread on the table, and pours olive oil and balsamic vinegar on each of their side plates.

Daugherty smiles and glances at the menu.

"It's very nice of you to be concerned about me and take me out for dinner. Please, allow me to pay for myself."

"This is kind of a working dinner, since I have some questions to follow up on, so please, this is on me or on the police department."

Reluctantly, Carly says, "Okay."

Daugherty sets down his menu. "So, you had a rough day? Wanna talk about it? I listen well."

Carly pauses. *Do I want to share such private information*? "Well, it doesn't relate to my case." Tears well up in Carly's eyes, stung by unexpected and intense emotions. With an ache gnashing at her stomach, Carly had hoped not to venture too deep. "Not right now. Maybe later." She forces a smile, then returns to the menu.

"I'm sorry you are distressed," Detective Daugherty says in an attempt to comfort. He reaches across the table to hold one of her hands.

Carly pulls away. "Do you have any information you can tell me about my past? I'm really upset about all of this on one level, 'cause I don't remember most anything. *That* bothers me, and I'm really upset that not only is my memory gone, but also that I don't have a lot of feelings about new things I'm uncovering. I mean, I keep hoping I'll wake up and realize I've just been in one long, bad dream."

"Sorry to hear," Daugherty says, trying to be supportive.

"It's not your fault. Why are you saying sorry?"

"I know, I'm just saying, I feel your pain. My sister was assaulted when she was fifteen, and I wish I could have been there to protect her. I'm sorry for what I know someone did. I relate to *that*." Detective Daugherty thoughtfully pauses. "She committed suicide a few years later because she couldn't deal with all the pain. I just wish I could have been there for her. She was one of the reasons I became a policeman."

Shaking her head, Carly says, "That's so sad."

After an awkward silence, Carly queries, "So, Detective...."

"Call me John."

Carly smiles. "Okay, John. Tell me, have you done any more investigating into my past or how I got to where I was? Anything you can share? I had wanted to pick your brain and see if it will help me or at least answer some questions."

"Anything specific you're wondering? I mean, I've looked at a lot of information. I know places you worked. I know about your husband and daughter. I know about your parents and immediate family. I know where you grew up and went to school. I know you used to attend a church, which was a kind of orthodox Christian church in your hometown, where you met and married your husband. I know you're an artist, like jazz music and fish. And I know you like Italian food."

"What do you know about my family? Where did I grow up? Where did I go to school?"

Detective Daugherty raises his hand up in front of him, in a stop motion, and smiles. "Woah, slow down. Some of this relates to an ongoing investigation, and I don't know how much I should really be sharing, legally, if not ethically."

"That's what my therapist said too, but if I keep getting little pieces of my past, maybe it will all click into place, like a big puzzle."

Just then their server, her face shining behind a habitual smile, approaches. "Good evening. My name is Francesca, and I'll be your server. Would you like something to drink?"

"Water is fine for me," Detective Daugherty says.

"I'd like a glass of Merlot." Carly smiles faintly at the waitress.

"I changed my mind. I'll have a glass of this." Daugherty chuckles, pointing to the wine list. "Cabernet, thanks."

"Have you all decided what you want to eat?"

"The roast duck sounds good. I think I'd like that."

"And for you, sir?"

"I'll have the same."

"Very good. Can I start you with a salad or soup?"

"What's your soup today? Do you have any specials?"

"Our soup of the day is *minestra di ceci*, which is a slight variation of minestrone made with chickpeas."

"Sounds delicious. I'll have a cup of the soup."

Carly says, "I'll have a chopped salad with Italian dressing on the side."

"I'll bring those right out."

After the waitress leaves, Detective Daugherty says, "Where were we? Let's see, you grew up in a little town north of New Brunswick and went to school in the same town–Oberton. Does that sound familiar?"

"No." Carly shakes her head. "I don't remember that."

"I can tell you that we don't have any solid leads. We've followed up on everything so far. No one saw anything, heard anything, or knows anything."

"What about any of my relatives, my family? Can you tell me about anyone or anything you found out that wouldn't compromise your investigation, like any more details about my life?"

"Well, from what I uncovered, your mom and dad both died of natural causes. You have a brother and a sister, both of whom don't live nearby. I'm still working on tracking them down."

A waiter delivers their wine, soup, and salad. "Enjoy."

"God, I'm starving," Carly says, digging into her salad. "I only had an apple for lunch. I wasn't that hungry, but I am now."

"This soup is delicious. Here, try some." Detective Daugherty offers Carly a spoonful of the soup.

"No thank you." Carly sips her wine then hangs her head.

"What's wrong? Is your wine okay?"

Carly hesitates and tilts her head. "Well, during therapy, I connected with a memory of seeing my little girl. I must have found her when…when she died. Is there anything you can tell me about the circumstances of her death or my husband's death?"

Dropping his head and taking in a big breath, Daugherty reluctantly states, "Um, well, I know some details, but this isn't really...."

"Detective, please."

Daugherty shakes his head and sighs. "All right. Your daughter was...," he pauses, "assaulted and murdered, and a couple months later your husband committed suicide. We don't really know a lot about why."

A lump once again forms in Carly's throat, as she recalls the image of her daughter. The memory rends her heart, hollowing out her soul. "On second thought, you know, I don't think I want to talk about this anymore."

"I'm sorry."

There is a long silence.

With a big breath, Carly states, "I've gotten a couple more calls I've been meaning to tell you about."

"What kind of calls?"

"Harassing calls like the other one I had gotten before I came down to the station."

"Was it a man or a woman? What did they say?"

"Well, it was a man...."

"Do you think, did it sound like the same guy who left the other message? What did he say?"

"In the first message the man just said he was watching me and asked if I was scared. In the next one he said we had unfinished business. The most recent one the person asked if I knew who he was."

Agitated by this news, Daugherty asks, "Why didn't you say something?"

"I *am* saying something now."

"Yeah, but I meant sooner."

"Maybe because it keeps happening in the middle of the night, so I guess I just put them out of my mind and forget about them."

"How many messages have you gotten? Did you save them?"

"No, I erased them. I didn't like them. I just wanted them gone. The last one upset me, so I changed my voice message asking the person to stop calling me."

"When you get home, you need to erase that. You don't want to antagonize someone like this. Let us handle it. I'm gonna tell Detective Jim. If you get any other calls, don't erase them."

"I thought you all were gonna put a tap on my phone."

"The order from the judge hasn't come through yet–bureaucratic red tape."

Carly sighs. "Okay, let's just enjoy our meal. No more questions. No more talk of awful stuff and awful people. Let's try to let this go for now."

Carly signals the waitress. "Excuse me, can I get a double shot of tequila, chilled with lime and salt, please?"

***

As they arrive back at Carly's apartment building, Detective Daugherty says with a smile, "Let me walk you to your door."

"Thank you, but I'm okay," Carly, states, desiring to distance herself from the detective. I promise when more memories come back, you'll be one of the first people I call."

"I'm sorry you had such a rough day. Things will get better. There is an old saying, I think applies here. 'This too will pass.' I'd like to think you're a happy-go-lucky artist normally."

"Thank you for dinner, Detective." Carly turns and politely, but abruptly ends the interaction, leaving Detective Daugherty standing outside the front entrance to the building.

"Night," he states, nodding, watching her disappear into the building.

CHAPTER TWENTY-SEVEN

ANOTHER CALL

With sleep eluding her once again, Carly rolls around in bed, her thoughts racing with the details of her life uncovered that day.

This just keeps getting worse. Maybe I really don't want to know the truth.

Carly drowses, her eyelids heavy.

Startled by the ringing phone, Carly reluctantly gets up and walks into the living room. The clock blinks back at her–3:07 a.m. Carly huffs.

A now-familiar voice whispers, "I'm watching you. You got away from me before but you won't next time. Don't mention this call to the police. I know you've been talking to them."

Carly's heart races.

I got away from him last time? If this guy is watching me and wants to hurt me, why hasn't he done something other than make idle threats? I need to tell the detective, but if I do, maybe he'll get hurt. If I don't, maybe I will.

Carly calls the police station. "Hi, may I speak to Detective Daugherty?"

"He's not here, ma'am. Would you like to leave him a message?"

"Yes, thank you."

Detective Daugherty's somewhat-geeky message plays: "I'm away from my desk or on the phone. Please leave a message for Detective Daugherty after the beep, and may the New Brunswick Police Force be with you."

Carly takes a deep breath, hoping she's doing the right thing. "Detective, it's Carly. I received another phone message. The guy said he was watching me. He said that I had gotten away last time but that I wouldn't get away again. He said not to tell the police, and that he knows I've been speaking with you. He never said my name, but this message seems different. I'm afraid this might be the guy who hurt me. I saved the message. What should I do now?" Sighing deeply, she hangs up.

I don't feel like sleeping at all now.

CHAPTER TWENTY-EIGHT

MORE SESSION NOTES

Carly struggles to fall back asleep, adrenaline coursing through her veins like flash flooding. Ruminations abound. She mindlessly clicks through a series of '80s reruns, infomercials, and sports highlights, seeing nothing of interest. She turns off the TV, reaches for Dr. Mentes' therapy session notes, then pauses, concerned after her recent session and discussion with Detective Daugherty what she might find. She pushes past her unease, taking the folder and opening to where she left off.

> May 28, 1997: Patient, Carly McCulley–Continuing Diagnosis–PTSD, dysthymia, schizoid issues, insomnia, nightmares. Verbatim transcription of this date's therapy session follows:
>
> **Dr. Mentes**: How are you today? I'd like to do an exercise from John Bradshaw's *Homecoming*.
>
> **Carly**: Okay, why are we doing this?
>
> **Dr. Mentes**: It's an exercise to assist you in leaving home, figuratively. I think some part of you is stuck in your family-of-origin home space. If this makes sense to you.

Carly: Um. Could you explain it?
Dr. Mentes: This is kind of like a badly scratched CD, skipping and playing the same thing over and over. In the same way, I think you're stuck or your inner child is stuck in time. Remember I previously asked you to look around when we were discussing the home you grew up in and asked who was there who loved you?
Carly: Yes. There was no one there who loved me. I never felt safe anywhere with anyone. I felt like I wasn't worthy to breathe and take up space. At my core, I feel like no one wanted me around, ever.

Sadness drags Carly down as she grieves for these forgotten memories and a dark foreboding invades her mind.

Dr. Mentes: I think this exercise will help you move out of *that* past. It's as if you're being held prisoner there by the trauma you don't remember and maybe never will remember. Does this sound okay?
Carly: I guess so.
Dr. Mentes: Did you bring that picture of yourself when you were young?
Carly: Yes. Here.
Dr. Mentes: What a beautiful, precious little girl you were. How old were you?

Carly's tears well up reading this. Pain bubbles up as she connects with the realization of not being loved, on a visceral level, even if the memory eludes her grasp.

> **Carly**: About five or six, maybe seven. I'm not sure.
> **Dr. Mentes**: I want you to focus on this time when you were this age. Was there anywhere around there during this time you felt safe?
> **Carly**: Kind of. I felt safe over at my cousin's house, who lived next door. Actually it was outside in her backyard.
> **Dr. Mentes**: Take a few moments to think back and remember this little girl and how she felt. Remember the house you lived in. Okay, sit back, close your eyes.

Carly skips past the now-familiar hypnosis directions, eager for answers.

> **Dr. Mentes**: When you get to the door with number one on it, open it. You see your house where you grew up. Look around and see everything. See the furniture. See your bedroom. Observe the color of the paint and the curtains. Notice how everything smells. Look at the floors and the ceiling. Walk through the house, the kitchen. Again, observe the color of the paint and the curtains, the sink, the stove, the refrigerator. What color the floor is. Is it tile, or carpet or something else? Notice how everything looks.

As Carly reads this, pain starts in the pit of her stomach, building inside her, like a volcano poised to erupt.

> **Dr. Mentes**: Envision yourself as an adult standing out on the front porch waiting for your five-year-old self to come and join you–as an adult. Now walk out the front door and as you do notice your mom and dad standing there smiling, and your younger self is in between them. Beckon to your younger self to walk over to you–as an adult. As your younger self comes over and stands next to you–as an adult, put your arm around your younger self, smile down at her and say, 'I love you, little Carly. I'm here for you, and I'll take care of you now.'

Carly's sadness explodes at these words, choking her. Trying to maintain her composure she blinks back tears, but continues reading, even as anguish wells up inside her as she considers having said these words to her inner child. *'I love you, little Carly. I'm here for you, and I'll take care of you now.'*

> **Dr. Mentes:** Now, you both wave to your mother and father and turn and walk away. I want you to walk over to your cousin's backyard, where you feel safe.
> **Transcriptionist interjects**: Sound of patient crying, as if she is having trouble catching her breath for an extended period of time (several minutes).

From an unknown place inside herself, Carly gives into the agony and bawls, yet somehow still feels detached. *This is not my reality.*

Dr. Mentes: Carly, what happened?
Carly: When I was putting my arm around Little Carly, I felt a huge, painful lump in the back of my throat. I had to choke down the horrible feelings that felt so deep and bad and strong and just…bottomless. They seemed to be part of me…my very essence. I kept thinking I cannot mess up what Dr. Mentes is doing here until I couldn't hold it in any longer. Once I walked to the place where you suggested I'd be safe, I couldn't hold those feelings down any longer and they just rushed out from a place so deep within me that I felt like my insides were getting ripped out.

Carly weeps uncontrollably. As sadness threatens to engulf and drown her, she sits in her spot by the bay window and pulls her knees up close to her body, wrapping her arms around them in a protective hug. *Isn't there any happiness in my life*?

CHAPTER TWENTY-NINE

MEETING

Carly wakes, still drowsy from sleep, sunlight streaming through the blinds. She notices the red light blinking on her answering machine. Her stomach tightens.

"Hi, Carly, this is Detective Daugherty. I got your message. Call me when you can. I want to talk to you about the voice messages."

Relief sweeps over Carly at hearing Daugherty's message.

***

Carly calls Detective Daugherty and the front desk officer transfers the call.

"Good afternoon. This is Detective Daugherty."

"Hi, it's Carly McCulley. It's afternoon already?"

"Yes, and remember, please call me John."

"Okay. John."

"So, tell me about the most recent message. What was said, exactly?"

"Not sure I remember exactly, but like I said in my message to you, the caller said he was watching me in the first message. In the second call he referred to having 'unfinished business,' I think, and that he was watching me. Well, this last call was more threatening. He said I got away before but that I wouldn't get away again. He didn't say my name or leave his name. He warned me not to call the police or talk to the police."

"It's good you called me. Why don't you come down to the station and bring your answering machine. You'll need to file a complaint about the harassing phone calls. Get here as soon as possible."

"Um, file a complaint? I'm not sure I want to do that. That'll turn this into a thing. I'm not sure I want this to turn into a *thing*."

"You need to come in, let us listen to the message, and get something on file so we can initiate some kind of...I don't know what, exactly, but so we can take more steps to protect you."

Carly pauses, uncertain how to proceed. She wishes the calls would just stop, but unless she did something, she doubted they would. "What about 3:30?"

"Okay. Would you like me to pick you up?"

"No. I can get there on my own."

"Okay, but in the meantime, I'm gonna see if I can get a couple extra uniforms to keep a closer eye on you."

"Thanks. This means a lot."

"I'll see you at 3:30. Be safe."

"I will. Goodbye, Detective."

Carly disconnects, dropping her phone on the sofa. After a few bounces, it settles upside down on one of the cushions. Carly remains still, staring at her phone, as if expecting it to ring any moment, to hear the breathy, gravel-laden voice on the other end with another escalation. She hopes he hasn't grown brazen enough to knock on her door, though the uniformed officers should deter him. *Will they be enough?*

CHAPTER THIRTY

INTERROGATION

Carly again parks in the large lot a block from the police station. She enters. The sharply dressed police officer sitting at the front desk looks up, acknowledging her presence.

Carly says, "I'm here to see Detective Daugherty from the Special Victims Unit."

"What's your name?"

"Carly McCulley. He is expecting me."

"I'll let him know you're here. Please take a seat."

"Thank you."

Detective Daugherty enters the waiting area and extends his hand to Carly, smiling. "How are ya doing? Come with me."

After taking a deep breath, Carly says, "I'm really upset about so many things."

As they walk up to the same windowless conference room they were in once before, Carly recognizes Jim Franklin, the detective she met on her previous visit. He extends his hand in greeting, smiling.

Detective Daugherty says, "Carly, Jim has a few more questions for you."

"Hi, Ms. McCulley."

Carly takes his hand. "Hello. I thought I was just coming down here to deliver my answering machine, so that you all could listen to the most recent message, and I'd be filing a complaint."

"Well, I have a couple more questions, if you don't mind. Do you remember anything new that you didn't tell us before prior to waking up in the hospital?"

"Like I said before, everything's fuzzy. I think I remember going to buy a bottle of wine and that's about it. Then I woke up in the hospital," Carly states sharply.

"I have to ask you again; you don't remember where you were or what you were doing, or who you were with the Friday night prior to ending up in that parking lot?" The question seems pointed and harsh to Carly.

Carly stares down at her hands, feeling defensive as if she is being interrogated. "Like I said before, I don't have much memory of anything. Other than what I told you before."

"You don't remember how you got to the parking lot at the 7-Eleven or how you got in the condition you were in?" Detective Franklin again poses the pointed questions.

Carly, unsettled, shakes her head and stares defiantly at Detective Franklin.

Daugherty queries, "Did you bring your answering machine?"

"Yes," she curtly replies as she retrieves it from inside her big leather bag, feeling on edge from the questioning. "I thought you all were going to tap my phone?"

"Yes, well the wheels of justice move slowly sometimes," Detective Franklin states, sounding slightly sarcastic.

Carly hands her answering machine to Detective Franklin, who states, "Thank you. Do I have your permission to listen to this and make a copy of the recording?"

"Yes."

Jim turns to Daugherty, motions with his hand. "John. Come with me."

Detective Daugherty states, "Stay here, we'll be right back. We're going upstairs to put this together."

After a few minutes, anxiety grips her. Carly steps out into the hallway to walk off her nerves. She passes a room and sees pictures on the wall. She backtracks and enters, finding herself in another long, dreary windowless conference room. It contains a few leather-covered office chairs, folding chairs, and several folding tables, with six large-sized bulletin boards hung end to end along the walls.

There are dozens of garish photos hung with push pins, while numerous other photos lay strewn out on the tables, all in a seemingly systematic fashion. There are notes and notepads, pens and clipboards, black and yellow markers and dozens of manila file folders filled with documents interspersed among the many photographs. The smell of stale coffee and futile desperation fill Carly's senses.

This is Homicide's war room.

The meticulously organized yet gruesome photos grouped by victim, capture Carly's interest. She's mesmerized.

The first group of photos are of a man, his skin grayish blue in death. There are shallow depressions where his eyes should be. Across each depression, crisscrossing in the middle, are two pieces of thick, black twine stitched diagonally in an *X*.

What happened to his eyes?

The same twine tacks his mouth shut, with a running cross-stitch. The area around each stitch is swollen, making it nearly impossible to see the twine. Carly notices a note:

> *It appears the victim's penis was cut off with something like a metal cutter and stuffed inside his mouth before it was sewn shut. Wounds were filled with salt. This was done perimortem.*

A jagged, haphazard scar slices through the area around the victim's wrist. Bones protrude from the garish stump. She sees another note:

> *It appears the perp cut off and stuffed the severed hand into the victim's anus. Definitely perimortem.*

Carly notices the man's feet are also missing, reading the description on the adjacent note:

The victim's toes were individually cut off one by one and the foot cut in half, then cut off above the ankle, all showing varying degrees of hemorrhagic staining in the surrounding tissue. These were subsequently stuffed in the victim's anus.

Carly stares, at once horrified and yet also entranced, feeling an unexpected anger rising inside her.

As she walks around the room, she gazes at more photos, spotting another man with the same pattern of having his eyes and mouth sewn shut, and his right hand cut off. Then another and another.

The next victim is an older woman. Similar injuries, but it appears her face was beaten on the right cheek, and her right hand appears to be crushed. With her pulse quickening, Carly reads the note below the photo:

Female victim's vagina sewn shut, stuffed with salt. It appears she was still alive when this occurred.

Strings run from each individual victim's board to a central board positioned above all the rest, with questions posited.

Do they work together?
Are they related?
How are they connected?
Do they have the same types of injuries?

Were all of these injuries perimortem or some postmortem?
What is our suspect's profile?
The victims:

1. *All had records.*
2. *All had been arrested for child abuse and death of a child under their care.*
3. *All had one or more children under their care with allegations of abuse, who were either removed from their care or who had died under suspicious circumstances.*

Carly shudders, trepidation and rage enveloping her mind and stifling her reason.

This guy is after me? What did I do to deserve this? How did I piss this guy off?

She feels uneasy as she reviews the list again. *All these victims had one thing in common: child abuse. Why is he after me?*

"Ah, ma'am."

Startled, Carly yelps, and turns to see Detectives Daugherty and Franklin in the doorway.

"You're not supposed to be in here," Detective Franklin states in a harsh matter-of-fact way.

"Sorry. You two were gone so long. I was just stretching my legs and looking for some water, then saw this room. You think the guy who's done all this is after me?" she asks incredulously.

Detective Daugherty responds, "Yes, but–"

"We *cannot* discuss this," Detective Franklin emphatically states.

"Why would he be after *me*?"

"Sorry, Ms. McCulley," Franklin states, with steel in his voice. "We cannot discuss this. We really need to move back into Interrogation Three."

"I think I have a right to know about someone like this trying to hurt me."

"You can't remember anything?" Detective Franklin prods again. "You don't know why this guy would want to harm you?"

Carly stares at her hands, imagines them gone, leaving nothing but stumps. She shakes her head.

Franklin blurts, "Did you ever abuse your daughter?"

Shocked and outraged, Carly barks out in response, "What! No! I loved my daughter. I could never…." Trembling inside, she shakes her head.

"If you don't remember, how do you know for sure?"

Daugherty steps in between them. "Jim, this may not be the best–"

"Not now, Daugherty." Franklin turns to Carly. "I'm sorry, but I had to ask."

"Well, I don't remember, but I am *not* a child abuser!" Carly spits out her response, overcome with anger, frustration, and indignation.

"I just have to wonder why our guy would be after you, when the one thing that the victims have in common is that they were child abusers and had children under their care who died under suspicious circumstances."

Again, Carly struggles not to burst out crying. "If there is nothing else, I'm leaving."

Franklin shakes his head, "I don't have any more questions for you. We're going to increase the undercover surveillance on you, having someone keep an eye on you 24/7."

Detective Daugherty says, "Let me walk you out."

As they walk out, Daugherty continues, "I didn't realize he was going to ask you those questions or talk to you that way. He didn't share that with me beforehand."

Walking next to him, Carly stares at the ground, saying nothing.

"Call me if you need anything." Daugherty states in an apparent attempt to offer a modicum of comfort.

Carly remains silent.

As Carly exits the police station and walks to her car, tears sting her eyes. Once inside the car, she sobs uncontrollably, resting her head on the steering wheel. Obsession replaces sadness as she replays the image of Elizabeth's dead body. *Why am I a target?*

CHAPTER THIRTY-ONE

MORE QUESTIONS

Carly leans up against a few pillows in the bay window. She stares at her phone. She debates calling her cousin, Sarah. Part of her wants to find out from someone who knows her, if she thinks her capable of hurting her child. Part of her doesn't really want the answer. She pulls her legs up close to her, then calls her cousin.

"Hi, Sarah. This is Carly." Her voice quivers. "Is this a good time to talk? I have some more questions. How are you doing, by the way?"

After a moment of silence, "I'm doing okay. I have some time. What's up? Is everything okay?"

Carly takes a breath. "How well do you know me, or do you know if I was a good person or not?"

"What are you getting at?"

Carly sighs. "Do you think I was a child abuser? Did I hurt my daughter? Was I responsible for her death somehow?"

"Hun, sweetie. First of all, I'm ninety-nine percent sure you loved your little girl with all your heart. I remember talking to you right after she was born. You were on cloud nine in love with her. While asking for advice on how to do this, you related that you wanted to make sure she knew she was loved and learn to trust you and that you would be there for her. When she'd wake up and cry, and you'd be delayed getting to her even a little bit, you'd call out to her from wherever you were, saying, 'Mommy's coming.'"

Hearing this, tears well up in Carly's eyes as she senses the truth of these words.

Her cousin continues, "I don't think someone who was an abuser would act like that. You told me when you got into therapy that one of the reasons was because you had a lot of anger bubbling up, but you didn't know why, and you didn't want to take it out on your daughter in any fashion. Second, someone molested her, and you wouldn't have had anything to do with that! Ever! Do you hear me? Some evil, selfish man did that, objectified her for his pleasure or anger or whatever it is that motivates creeps that do those things."

Carly nods in agreement. "Yeah." Her anger burns hot, listening to her cousin recount the circumstances around Elizabeth's death.

"He didn't look at her as a precious little girl with feelings. I know this is hard to deal with, but you didn't have anything to do with that."

A chill runs the length of Carly's spine.

"What's going on?" Sarah asks. "Where did this question come from?"

"The police asked. You know, I'm not sure I wanna talk about it. I feel like it's taking all my energy to hold it together right now. Thank you for the answers and your kindness."

"You're welcome. Are you sure you don't want to talk some more? I'm a good listener. You know, I'm actually trained to do that."

"No. I don't think so. Not at the moment."

"Just know, I'm here for you."

"Thank you so much for your time."

"Whammi hugs. Bye."

"Thank you. Bye." Carly hangs up, comforted at her cousin's words, awash with a modicum of relief, but one thought casts shadows on her mind.

A serial killer is after me. Why?

CHAPTER THIRTY-TWO

ENOUGH

Another threatening phone call greets Carly upon her return from the store.

"I'm gonna get you. You got away from me, but you won't get away again. I hope this scares you. I'll be seeing you soon."

Enough!

Carly changes her voice message.

"Hi. You've reached Carly. Please leave a message after the tone, unless you're the chicken-shit coward who keeps calling and trying to threaten me. I don't know why you're harassing me! Meet me at the library tomorrow at noon. All I keep hearing is a lot of empty, bullshit threats! I'll be at the center lunch table out in front of the library with a red blouse on. You should be able to find me easily."

She stops the recording, her heart racing. She reaches for the erase button, but decides to leave the message.

She dials another number.

"Hello, is Detective Daugherty in?"

"He's not available. Would you like his voicemail?"

"Sure."

The receptionist transfers Carly.

A computerized message comes on the line: "After the tone, please leave a message for extension 3122."

"That's odd." *I wonder if he changed his message.*

"Detective–John–it's Carly. I just received another threatening call. I've had enough! I changed the message on my answering machine. I'm calling the creep out to meet me in front of the library at noon tomorrow. You all can look after me with the cavalry ready to come to the rescue. I have the feeling this guy's bark is a lot worse than his bite," Carly snaps. "I bet he doesn't even show."

Carly hangs up. Unsettled somehow, she's having a hard time putting her finger on why. That the voicemail for Detective Daugherty had changed nags at her.

CHAPTER THIRTY-THREE

ANTICIPATION

After Carly leaves the message for Detective Daugherty, she telephones Robert. *I need to go have some fun.*

"Robert, it's Carly, can we get together Friday or Saturday? There's a new art opening down at the museum, or maybe we can just get together for a night in? I'll make you something special. We can put on an old movie, just hang out and relax."

"Not Friday, I have my little girl."

Carly's heart sinks, her face flushing with embarrassment. "Oh, sorry, I didn't–"

"Saturday's good though. Wanna come over about 7:30? we can cook or order take out. We'll just hang out, no pressure. I know you want to move slowly."

"Sounds wonderful. Let's just get together and enjoy each other's company."

"Sounds good."

"See you then." Carly ends the call. A rush of excitement fills her, replacing the shame from a moment ago.

She wishes she could remember more about Robert, something to connect them before the attack.

The current feelings she has for him will have to do, for now.

CHAPTER THIRTY-FOUR

MEETING FATE

Anxiety washes over Carly as she gets dressed. *What am I doing*? *Maybe I should just let the police do their thing. These maddening phone calls have to stop*!

A short time later, she pulls into an open spot in the New Brunswick Civic Center parking garage, relieved to see a lot of cars and people out and about.

Carly waits for a group of people before heading for the stairwell to the ground level and follows them down, thankful for safety in numbers, then walks toward the library, her dread increases with every step.

The huge, three-story mortar-and-stone library boasts over 50,000 books and faces an expansive plaza, strewn with brightly colored, canopy-covered tables nestled among towering oak trees, intermittently sprinkled with old stone tables embossed with chessboards. At the center of the plaza, an impressive fountain bubbles, graced by three partially nude statues standing back-to-back, each bending slightly at the waist, forever pouring water from their down-turned pitchers. *Drink from the Endless Knowledge Inside* is engraved at their feet.

On the center lawn area, children kick soccer balls and chase each other playing tag or throwing footballs, while scattered picnickers bask in the sun. Dozens of pigeons and sparrows scavenge for food. Black wrought-iron benches encircle the central grassy areas where people of all ages gather–sitting, watching, participating, waiting, and eating handcrafted foods, from falafels, tacos, hot dogs, and assorted nuts to ice cream cones in various flavors and colors. Three gourmet coffee vendors are scattered throughout the area in portable kiosks. The air on any given day is a sumptuous mixture of exotic pipe smoke from the old masters facing off at chess, fresh-brewed coffee, roasted hazelnuts, and mouthwatering fried foods.

This area and these scents conjure pleasant feelings for most, but today Carly's anxiety deepens with every breath. She walks over to the closest food vendor. "May I get a Chicago dog and an iced coffee, please?"

"Do you want everything on the dog?"

"Yes, please."

"Would you like an extra shot of espresso?"

"No, just the regular. Thank you."

"That'll be $5.50."

Carly strolls to one of the center tables and sits, eyeing the passersby. She carefully unwraps the hot dog so as not to spill the peppers and sweet-pickle relish. *These are so messy, but so good.*

After she finishes the hot dog, she sits with her back to the library, takes out her sketch pad and, facing the courtyard where most of the people are located, considers what to sketch first.

No one looks suspicious. I doubt this guy will show up. I don't see any police. They are probably undercover.

Carly sketches some children dressed in colorful outfits, playing with their moms on the swings and slide. The minutes turn into an hour, then two hours.

Finally, at three o'clock, a boy with sandy-blond hair riding on a skateboard approaches. "Is your name Carly?"

"Yes."

"I was told to give this to you." The boy hands Carly a folded piece of paper and skateboards away.

"Wait, who gave this to you?"

Carly looks at the paper. On each side the word *over* is written. After she turns the paper over a couple times, she looks around the area, panic creeps over her, smothering her like a pillow held over her face.

Where are the police? *Why didn't someone swoop down and apprehend or at the least stop the boy*? *Maybe that only happens in the movies. What if this person is watching me right now*? *Oh God, what do I do*?

Carly rushes into a hall by the restrooms inside the library, desperately searching for Detective Daugherty's number in her purse. Alarm overwhelming her reason, she misdials the number three times. "Hi, I'd like to speak with John, er, Detective Daugherty, please."

"May I ask who's calling?"

"It's Carly McCulley." Carly watches anyone entering the building or looking at her. Paranoia seizes and slows her brain.

"Just one moment, ma'am." The receptionist transfers Carly.

"This is Detective Daugherty, may I help you?"

"Oh, thank God. It's Carly. Did you get my message I left about meeting the guy who was leaving messages on my machine?"

"No, when did you leave it?"

"Yesterday afternoon."

"Where are you?"

"The library."

"Wait, what? You went to the library to meet the guy who's been leaving you threatening messages?"

Carly detects panic in his voice.

"Yes. I'm inside the library. He was supposed to meet me at noon, but no one showed. Then this boy came up to me and gave me a note that had the word *over* written on both sides of it. Shortly after getting the note, I realized this was a stupid idea and came inside the library. I'm really scared."

"Don't move. I'll be there to pick you up. Meet me outside at the popcorn vendor. Don't go to your car. There's a chance the guy doesn't know your car, and we don't want to lead him to it. I'll have a plainclothes officer go get your car and take it to the station. You can pick it up from there. Stay put."

Carly goes outside and walks over to the popcorn vendor.

"May I help you?" the man at the cart asks.

"Um, no, thank you." She moves away, eyeing the man.

After what seems like an excessive amount of time, Detective Daugherty's car pulls up, lights flashing. She runs to it.

"Oh my God, thank you, this was really stupid."

"Give me your keys. I need to give them to the officer to get your car. I'll be right back, stay put."

After a minute the detective gets back in the car. "I agree that this wasn't the best idea."

"These anti-anxiety meds and pain meds mixed tequila have made me crazy. I'm so sorry. I just had had enough! This isn't helping you protect me."

"You've been under a lot of stress. Let's get you home."

"Thanks. I'll be okay. I have a date with Robert. I'll stay put until then. I'll be safe."

"Well, we have surveillance in place. We'll be looking out for you."

"Thank you. I appreciate it."

Carly considers the continual police presence. The protection gives her a sense of security, but she can already feel them watching, which makes her equally uneasy. The paranoia of the afternoon returns, distressing her.

CHAPTER THIRTY-FIVE

SECOND DATE WITH ROBERT

Carly changes her clothes a half dozen times, finding at least one thing wrong with each outfit. *I don't like how any of these look. I want to look great.* She settles on a sleeveless, peach-colored sundress covered with white print flowers and a cream-colored lightweight sweater.

Even though she is wary of strangers, she decides to take a cab to Robert's loft. As she exits and pays the driver, butterflies take flight in her stomach. *Why am I so nervous? This is good.* She stops to calm herself as she walks up to the elevator and pushes the button to the top floor. *Remember to breathe.* When the doors open into Robert's loft, she's greeted with the yummy smell of spaghetti sauce. The momentary flood of adrenaline stuns her. Feelings of desire leave her speechless upon seeing Robert. Lost for a moment, Carly stands motionless, trying to regain her composure. She trembles as Robert turns, looks at her, and moves toward her.

"You're breathtaking. You smell great and look great. We're just going to relax and have a good time. Don't worry, I'm going to be a total gentleman. Well, maybe not *total*, but we won't go anywhere or do anything you're not ready for, my lady." Robert smiles, takes one of her hands and kisses it.

Still stunned, Carly tries to smile.

"Let me get us something to drink," Robert continues. "I have what *I think* is a nice cabernet I found and wanted to share with you."

Carly breathes in deeply. "Yes, a drink, that would be nice. I'll put on some music."

"Sounds good. Here, I want you to taste the sauce."

Carly feels weak as she walks over to where Robert has moved next to the simmering spaghetti sauce. He holds a small wooden spoon up with some sauce on it and blows on it. "Do you approve? Do you think it needs anything?"

"It smells amazing." *Remember to breathe.* She tastes the sauce. "Yum. This is great. Maybe some more garlic, but then I love garlic, and maybe a little more wine. But really, it's good as is."

"As you say. Here, you doctor it, and I'll pour the wine."

Carly adds some powdered garlic and a little wine, stirring some, then tasting. "Perfect."

Robert takes out a wineglass, and after holding it up to the light, pours Carly a generous amount of wine. He hands the glass to her, then picks up his own glass. "I want to make a toast. Here's to us creating some amazing new memories together."

They clink glasses.

Carly takes a drink, pauses. "This is delicious."

"I'm happy you approve."

Carly lets the warmth from the wine circulate through her body. She walks over to Robert's high-tech stereo equipment with a vintage turntable and looks for some music. "What are you in the mood for?"

"I'm game, whatever you want."

Carly selects Dave Matthews'–*Crash*. "I think I like this CD." Carly says, smiling.

"*You* gave it to me."

Carly clicks the CD button to queue up "Crash Into Me." *This feels right.* As the first sweet strains of music fill the room, she says, "I thought this would be instrumental." Carly's jitters subside. She enjoys the movements of Robert's body while he cooks. *He's a beautiful man.* She just stands there admiring him.

Suddenly overcome with a rush of desire she leans against the counter to steady herself.

"There are a lot of other choices there."

"No, this is good. Great, actually. I feel like this is the first time, er...I mean...I'm...I'm just a bit nervous." *This song is appropriate.*

"I'm going to get the water ready for the spaghetti." Robert fills a pot with water and places it on the burner and sets a timer. Then he strolls over behind Carly, removes her sweater and gently lays it on the couch. As he places a hand on each of her shoulders and begins to massage them, he bends down and whispers, "Just relax. You're safe. Trust me."

At his touch, a bolt of lightning surges through Carly's body, causing her knees to weaken. Time stands still. Pleasure consumes her as reality slips away. She breathes in deeply and moans, trying to maintain her composure.

"I love the way you smell."

"You make my wees neak...I mean...." Carly giggles.

"You okay?"

"Um, yeah." She struggles to find the right word. "Fine, good. I'm good." She smiles.

The timer buzzes. "Let me go put the spaghetti in." Robert releases his grip on her shoulders. "I hope you're hungry."

Forget the food. I want more of this. Resembling a contented cat, Carly stretches her neck up with her eyes closed and sighs. She drinks some more wine. "Anything I can do?"

"Here, take this, and put it on the table."

Robert reaches out with the garlic bread. Carly takes the bread and puts it on the table, then moves toward Robert and caresses his arm, burying her nose between his body and his arm and breathes in. His musky smell sends shivers down her spine. She looks up at him. "You're simply beautiful." She wraps her arms around him and runs her finger along the outline of his body as if drawing a picture. "I want to remember you and never forget again." She takes one of his hands and turns it over, examining it. "You're just...magnificent."

Robert wraps his arms around her and lifts her off the floor, kissing her first on the lips, then on her face, then down her neck.

A confluence of desire and rushing emotions weakens Carly, as her body lights up.

Robert starts to say, "If we keep up like this, we'll...."

Carly responds as she gazes into his eyes. "Food can wait. Right now, I want you."

Robert moves the boiling water off the burner and states, "As you wish." As he caresses and kisses her neck, he nestles his face into her hair. He turns her around and unties the sundress straps, allowing the dress to drop to the floor.

As Carly closes her eyes, embracing the feelings, her breathing deepens. Carly turns and starts to help Robert out of his shirt.

"You're trembling. Are you okay?"

"I'm good." *Breathtaking.* Carly caresses the muscles on his arms and runs her fingers through his hair and down his back and kisses his chest.

Robert says, "I've missed you."

He turns Carly around once again, pushes her up against the wall, shoving the entire weight of his body against hers.

She feels the warmth of his breath and hears his breathing deepen, matching hers. "I want you. You take my breath away." He continues to kiss her neck.

Waves of pleasure surge through her body.

He backs away a step and finishes removing his shirt.

Carly turns around, watching him.

Robert embraces her again, kissing her.

Carly grabs his hand and pulls him up the stairs toward his bedroom. At the top of the stairs, she gazes into his eyes, removing her panties.

As Robert continues kissing her, she grabs his hair and presses up against him, pulling his head down so she can whisper in his ear, "I want you inside me."

Robert smiles and eagerly lays Carly down on the bed, gazing at her. He increases the intensity of his movement and presses his lips to hers. He rests his weight on his elbows, positioning her underneath him. He stretches her arms out above her head and holds them down with his full strength. Robert pauses, his breathing hastening, smiling. He kisses her deeply starting at her lips, slowly moving to her neck and down to her breasts.

Carly feels as though she's falling. *Is time standing still*? She wiggles out from underneath him, rolls and pushes him to the mattress, climbing on top of him, kissing and licking and nipping his skin with her teeth. She runs her hands and fingernails over Robert's biceps and back and down his sides.

Robert moans and lets out a deep breath. His breathing deepens. He once again moves on top, rolling the two of them, urgently kissing and squeezing Carly's breasts, taking each nipple in his mouth, continuing kissing and licking down to her abdomen, running his fingers along her sides as if playing a delicate instrument.

He reaches over to the drawer next to the bed and pulls out some soft white twine, fashioning a loop, "Are you okay with this?"

Carly hesitates, but nods.

He proceeds to wind the loops around Carly's wrists, pulls her arms up with the twine, then begins to tie them off at each corner of the headboard. Each tug sends an unwelcome wave of panic through Carly. She shudders, straining against the twine.

"You okay?"

Carly nods. *I need to let go and get out of my head.*

Robert continues kissing and caressing her neck and moves down to her nipples, first licking around them and then playfully biting the one on the right. Carly is hit by a wave of intense desire from her nipples down to her sweet spot. Suddenly she's flattened by a surge of anxiety-laden anger, even as her breath becomes shallow and her body throbs.

As Robert continues to kiss and lick down her abdomen and spreads her legs, Carly tries to sit up. Overwhelmed in a morass of arousal, anxiety, sadness, and disorienting anger, Carly pleads, "Stop. Please."

"Okay." Robert unties her.

"I'm sorry." Shaking her head. "I don't know what's wrong."

Robert tries to give Carly a reassuring hug.

Carly pulls away, quickly dressing. "I'm so sorry. I have to go. This is just…too much. I don't know what's wrong. I'm so sorry." Carly starts crying.

"It's okay." Robert attempts another hug.

She pulls away, holding her hand up. "Please, stop."

Nodding and motioning his hands, making an air hug, he kindly says, "Carly."

Disheveled and rushed, she heads for the door, leaving Robert on the bed. She hurries down the stairs, while throwing her dress on. The elevator's outer door sticks with the first pull, then whips open. Carly steps into the elevator, quickly closing the door behind her before Robert can follow. A tempest of feelings overwhelms her, exploding. *Goddammit*! *What the fuck is wrong with me*?

CHAPTER THIRTY-SIX

CONFUSED

A message from Robert greets her when she arrives home.

"Hey, it's me. Please, know I get this. I understand, or at least I think I understand, what you're going through. Maybe not exactly, but I'm sorry if I rushed us. This feels like something we worked through before when we first got physical. The first time we tried to have sex, you described that you had overwhelming feelings of the fear of a two-year-old, with the limited and confusing emotional development of a hormone-crazed teenager, in the nervous system of a full-grown woman. We worked through all that before. We can do it again. Whenever you're ready."

Hearing these words, Carly feels more lost and confused.

Robert's message continues. "You once shared a story about your mom. When you were about seven years old you asked her to sew the hem on your Brownie dress. You watched as she sewed a zigzag in one spot over and over again. You realized she was ill. You said it was at that point that you knew you really had no one you could count on to take care of you. I need you to hear me–you are not alone. I'm here for you. I care about you."

Carly is comforted and at the same time hot tears burn her cheeks as sadness threatens to overwhelm her. She saves the message and covers her eyes with her hands, trying to hide from the reality of it all.

Though Robert's message comforts her, hearing he's there for her, she wonders how much he can really help, how much anyone can.

She dials Dr. Mentes and leaves a message. "Dr. Mentes, this is Carly McCulley. I was wondering if I could get in to see you tomorrow. I'm really upset and confused and angry and sad and don't understand what's going on."

Sighing and taking a deep breath, Carly takes one of the Xanax that Dr. Mentes prescribed. She arranges the pillows on the seat in front of the bay window and scoots in among them, pulling her legs up next to her, as if the pillows were barriers protecting her, rendering her invincible in her favorite spot.

***

The ringing telephone jars Carly awake. Stumbling to the phone, she picks it up. "Hello."

"Carly, this is Dr. Mentes. You said you needed to come in for an appointment?"

She shakes off the drowsiness, running her fingers through her hair. "Yes, I was at my friend's house, and we were in the middle of having sex when I...I just kinda freaked out and had to leave. I feel awful.

I don't understand. I feel angry and sad and scared and confused. Normally I can think my way through things, but I...I need your help. I feel like I'm drowning."

"I have an appointment available first thing tomorrow. Can you wait until then? If this is an emergency, I have a colleague who I can refer you to."

"No, I want to see you. Tomorrow is okay."

"In the meantime, I want you to draw a picture of how you feel. Why don't you try that? Have little Carly, that part of you that's overwhelmed right now, illustrate how she feels. I'll see you tomorrow morning."

"Thank you, Doctor."

Carly hangs up, then collapses back into the pile of pillows. She stares at her ceiling fan, spinning on its slowest setting. She tries to focus on one blade, following its circumference around the housing, a slight wobble throws off its steady swirl.

She exhales, grateful for the call from Dr. Mentes, for the appointment in the morning, a life preserver keeping her afloat.

***

With low melodic notes of Robert Johnson facing the devil at the crossroads playing in the background, Carly picks up her drawing pad and pencil. *How do I feel? Little Carly, how do you feel? This is silly.* Carly struggles through a tangled tempest of terrible emotions. As she draws a picture of a little girl crying, she slowly becomes aware that the picture is of her inner child, little Carly, beaten up and badly bruised all over, just standing there, wearing only underpants, her hair a tangled mess. Intense anger overpowers Carly. She grits her teeth at the image. Pressing hard, digging a black line across the image with a charcoal pencil, she drags the pencil across the drawing, aggressively scrawling back and forth, crossing out the drawing.

This needs to be darker.

She grabs the darkest charcoal pencil and obliterates the picture with such force and fury her pencil snaps, shredding the paper.

Carly sobs. She slams the pencil down and swipes and rips the drawing from the desktop. She pounds her fists into a pillow, screaming at the top of her lungs, futilely attempting to discharge the overwhelming dark despair that has descended, threatening to swallow her whole. The rage stubbornly remains, surging through her, leaving her helpless.

CHAPTER THIRTY-SEVEN

ANOTHER NIGHTMARE

Carly walks through a house at night in utter darkness. A tsunami of fear and anxiety wash over her. People outside yell, wanting to kill her. Their disgust is palpable.

The scene changes to her driving her car, which morphs into a bicycle; the bicycle then transforms into a tricycle. She crashes into a kitchen. She notices a newspaper lying on the floor and reads its headline: "Carly Murdered." Torn up pieces of the paper litter the floor. She gets down on her hands and knees, crawling around, futilely trying to pick the shredded pieces of paper up off the floor. As she does, the black-and-white checkerboard tile melts into square holes. She falls into the basement. She notices the ceiling, the wood-frame boards resemble the cement roofing structure of a parking garage. She notices a car parked all alone. As she approaches, she realizes it is abnormally dark on one side and appears completely opaque. The darkness feels evil. As she attempts to peer inside of the car, fear suffocates her.

Breathing heavily, Carly wakes, sweating.

Just a bad dream.

As Carly lays there considering the dream, she suddenly has a memory flashback. She remembers the time, she had read about in Dr. Mentes' journal, when she was very young. She was climbing up on her dad's lap and telling him 'I love you daddy and I want to marry you.' The scene changes and she sees herself in the bedroom where her dad slept. He has his hand around the back of her neck. He thrusts his dick down her throat with such violence it jerks her head backwards.

Carly now fully awake, is at once stabbed with a piercing sorrow deep in her gut, drowns in the overwhelming feelings of such a massive betrayal of innocent trust, then explodes into a Vesuvius of venomous rage, that threatens to consumes her. She is again sickened with the reality of her life.

CHAPTER THIRTY-EIGHT

ANOTHER THERAPY APPOINTMENT

Carly approaches Dr. Mentes' office. She breathes in deeply, taking comfort in the familiar smell of lilacs.

She looks for the clipboard inside the office with only her name on the solitary piece of paper.

Carly reads the questions and responds.

How are you sleeping?

Badly, and having nightmares.

How are you feeling?

I feel like…I don't know what I feel. Angry, sad, anxious, tired, scared, depressed, knotted up, confused.

Any thoughts of suicide?

Nope.

Do you feel anyone is trying to hurt you?

Does a possible serial killer count? Does the nightmare count where people are trying to kill me?

Carly jots down her answers, then rings the bell and takes a seat to wait for Dr. Mentes.

After a few minutes, Dr. Mentes appears. "Hi, Carly. Come in and have a seat."

Carly smiles, the perfunctory grin she flashes when uncertain or afraid. She walks into Dr. Mentes' office and sits in the same comfy chair she always does, her back to the wall where she can see the door. Nervousness bites at her senses like a relentless gnat buzzing around, incessantly attacking its prey. *I'm a mess.*

Dr. Mentes glances down at the weekly depression questionnaire, asking, "So, what's going on?"

Carly tenses, her limbs rigid. "Um, I feel...I'm a mess. I dunno. I feel everything and nothing all at once."

Carly takes a deep breath. "I don't understand what's going on. I had a date with my friend Robert, and as we started to have sex, I was enjoying myself, but the more we got into it, I started to panic and then got angry. I felt like I couldn't catch my breath. I got so upset, I had to break it off and leave. Now, I feel confused and sad and angry and frustrated and guilty for running out the way I did. Then, last night, I had a really weird nightmare. I woke up overwhelmed with fear and felt like I couldn't breathe. And on top of all this, I've been angry–and I mean *extremely* angry–about *everything.* I've even felt angry at the air."

"Carly, given all you've been through, I'm not surprised you're having difficulty being intimate. Can you remember what you were thinking about when you panicked during sex?"

"I dunno. I was trying to stay out of my head. I was just trying to feel, to experience the moment. It was after he started to tie my wrists...." Carly pauses.

"Wait, he tied you up?"

"It was *just* twine." Carly considers this. "*Maybe* that *is* when I started to panic. Then he got close to touching my…vagina. Did I ever have a problem like this before? I mean, he was so sweet and trying to go slow and take his time. I just feel awful about this."

"First of all, we feel what we feel. Try not to layer feeling guilty about all this on top of trying to deal with what's going on with you."

Carly shakes her head, feeling downtrodden.

Dr. Mentes states, "At the very least, this sounds like feelings or even body memories from your distant past and recent past are colliding in the present with the fear related to all of that."

"What do you mean?"

"As a child, your trust was betrayed and you were molested by you father. Recently, you were badly beaten and severely injured. Who knows what this man, who the police say is a serial killer, said or did to you during that time. I think you said the injuries on your wrists indicated you'd been tied up."

Carly listens with sadness, staring down at the floor, hearing what Dr. Mentes was saying rings true.

"You were probably triggered by what Robert did. Subconsciously, your mind is aware of what happened to you, even if you cannot consciously remember it. It may very well be your memories are getting close to resurfacing."

Carly nods. "Actually, I just had a memory flash this morning. I remembered a time I was telling my dad I loved him and wanted to marry him." Carly starts to cry as she struggles to form the words to relate her recall while feelings overwhelm her senses. "The next thing I know I was back in his bedroom and he was ramming his cock down my throat so hard that my head was jerked backward." Carly chokes out the words intermixed with sobs that are welling up from the depth of her soul.

After pausing, Dr. Mentes states, "Having sex with one's partner is a powerful force Even if you don't remember what occurred when you were attacked recently, it could be that...what formerly was enjoyable for you with Robert, triggered the recall of the feelings related to that stranger assaulting you. Also, it seems these feelings are activating unresolved issues from your past, which is further complicating all of this."

As Carly's considers all Dr. Mentes is saying, crushing sadness continues. Tears stream down her cheeks.

"Didn't the police say you had had sex and that it most likely wasn't consensual?"

Carly responds weakly, "Yes."

"What you're experiencing is completely understandable. I don't know if that makes this any easier to accept."

Carly nods.

"Carly, one of your defense mechanisms to keep your pain at bay, is to intellectualize what is going on. There are some things, like pain, you cannot think your way past. You have to feel this. It may be scary. It may feel overwhelming, but I know you can deal with it." Dr. Mentes smiles with sympathy. "You're a strong woman. Your mind will let you recall all of this at some point, when you are ready."

"So, you're saying my memories may be getting ready to come back? And until I get to that place, I'm just going to keep feeling majorly fucked up like this?" Carly sighs, shaking her head.

"There is something we can use that may help. I would like to use a technique called EMDR. EMDR is an acronym for Eye Movement Desensitization and Reprocessing. When a person experiences a traumatic event, their feelings and memories get frozen and later become fused together with other similar events that occur subsequent to the initial event. Our feelings, memories and emotions get tangled up with the new related experience, making it feel more powerful and overwhelming than it really is. This is in essence PTSD.

"For example, when a war veteran hears a car backfire, they experience this as if they were hearing a gun being fired; their limbic system activates their amygdala which in turn causes their body to produce adrenalin. They have a fight or flight response to a car backfiring as if they were back in the original war situation; *as if* there was actually gunfire near them and their life was being threatened.

"EMDR allows us to untangle the feelings, memories and emotions that have gotten jumbled and hyperconnected. This allows a person to react to present moment events more normally. In the case of the soldier, when he hears a car backfire, it will just sound like a car backfiring. He won't think it's a gunshot and will end up fearing for his life.

"I would like to work with your recent memory recall about your dad. Do you feel up to trying this right now?"

Carly frowns skeptically. "Okay. What do I need to do?"

"Do you remember your safe space you created?"

"Um." Carly considers a moment. "I'm...not sure."

"I will want you to go in your mind to the safe spot when I say to go there."

"Refresh my memory, what is it again?"

Dr. Mentes refers to her notes and reads: "It's a secluded grotto in the middle of a forest, with a beautiful waterfall cascading down into a tranquil pool of crystal-clear water, surrounded by a collection of colorful stones lying just beneath the surface. Sunlight illuminates the landscape with subtle specs of gold and peach. The entire area emanates a rich and warm earthiness."

"Come sit here." Dr. Mentes rises and arranges two chairs, facing each other about two feet apart. She gestures to Carly to sit in one.

Carly sits opposite Dr. Mentes.

Dr. Mentes hands Carly two gray lead wires, each about six inches long, with cylindrical nodes on the end that are the width of a quarter. "Hold one of these in each hand. These will lightly vibrate, alternating between one hand and then the other. I will be asking you questions about your feelings. I want you to focus on your feelings, not the lead wires or the vibrations. Do you understand?"

"I think so."

"Think about what you shared with me." Dr. Mentes asks a series of questions, pausing momentarily between each question.

"Think about how you were feeling as you were telling your dad you loved him.

"Where were you in the house?

"How were you feeling?

"Was it day or night?

"Remember what you were saying."

Carly begins to cry as excruciatingly intense feelings well up inside her.

"On a scale of one to ten, how strong are these feelings right now?"

After pausing, Carly shakes her head and sadly states, "About eight or nine."

Carly senses the vibration of the nodes in her hands, first her right hand and then her left hand.

Dr. Mentes continues, "Remember that time.

"Was it day or night?

"What was the temperature in the room?

"Remember how you were feeling and what you were saying and doing."

As her emotions intensify, a lump forms at the back of Carly's throat. She weeps with an enormous force from deep inside herself, feeling the full impact of her dad's betrayal and grieving this insidious unnamed loss.

"Just stay with those feelings. You are doing great." Dr. Mentes pauses and allows Carly time to grieve. "Now I want you to go to your safe place. Take some deep breaths and relax."

Over the period of a few minutes, Carly notices the nodes' vibration lessen in intensity and then cease completely.

"How do you feel now, on a scale of one to ten?"

After a moment or two in her safe space, Carly calms. She gathers her thoughts. "About a three now I guess."

"That is good. Okay, now let's go back to those feelings that are a three. Think about what happened, what you said, how you felt."

Carly notices the nodes begin to vibrate again as she returns to the newly found and recently mollified memory. The feelings well up inside her once again. She weeps while feeling the unrestrained grief.

As Carly's sadness and tears diminish, Dr. Mentes directs, "I want you to go to your safe spot again. Take some deep breaths. What level is the pain now, on a scale from one to ten?"

Carly struggles to form words. "It's hard for me to get out of my feelings, because there are no words there. I guess the feelings are less than one now."

"Okay, tell me what words are coming up."

After searching and having a hard time conceptualizing what she is feeling, Carly states, "Confused I guess and…like…I'm in disbelief."

"This is exactly what I would expect a little child would be feeling. They are confused because they have no idea what is going on."

As Dr. Mentes states this, anger and rage boil up inside Carly. She spits out with disgust, "The fucking selfish bastard ruined my life! This is somehow connected to another memory that I just recalled, that doesn't seem related to the memory with my dad. It is a memory from when I was about 8 years old. Me and my dad and mom went to see my brother graduate from marine corps boot camp at Cherry Point, North Carolina. We were at a hotel and my mom was giving me a bath. The next thing I remember I was looking for her; she was outside sitting in our car. I called to her, but she wouldn't respond to me. She just sat there and stared straight ahead."

"What happened after that?"

With an overwhelming sense of dismay, Carly states, "I don't...remember...I don't know. I'm having a hard time describing what I feel...fear...dread, I guess lost, abandoned, betrayed. There is a dark elusive uneasiness I feel. When, as an adult, I try to consider what happened after I went back into the hotel room with my dad, my mind doesn't want to go there and I feel sick to my stomach and really anxious."

"How are you feeling now?"

"Really fucking angry." Carly starts crying again.

Dr. Mentes pushes a box of Kleenex over to Carly and pauses, allowing her time to settle.

Carly chokes through her sobs, shaking her head.

"Now, close your eyes and take a few deep breaths." Dr. Mentes pauses. "Keep in mind, this is not happening now. It happened. It's valid, but this is not happening now. It is in the past. Relax. Give yourself time. Do you remember that deep-breathing exercise I taught you?"

"I'm not sure."

"To do the deep breathing to help you relax, first close your eyes. Breath in deeply for a count of three. Hold your breath there for a count of three. Then breathe out for a count of three. Do this until you feel slightly weightless."

"Okay, I'll try that.

"So now tell me more about the nightmare you had last night. Did you have any strong feelings in the dream? Was there anything that kind of stood out in your mind from the dream, something that may have had significance or particular importance?"

Carly thinks for a minute. "Well, I was walking around a house in the dark. It was nighttime. People were chasing me, trying to kill me. It was kinda weird, because then I felt like I was driving, and the scene changed, and I felt like I was riding a bicycle, and then that changed into a tricycle, and I crashed into a kitchen.

"Does the kitchen seem familiar to you?"

"Yes, it's the house I grew up in."

"On the kitchen floor were wadded-up pieces of paper, like tissue or newspaper. I read a headline on the newspaper that I'd been murdered."

"Murdered?" Dr. Mentes leans in toward Carly, tilts her head and blinks as she queries.

"Yes, the headlines on the paper said that." Carly continues, "Next, I got on my hands and knees trying to pick up the pieces of balled up paper on the floor, when suddenly, the black squares in the kitchen floor that were part of a checkerboard design turned into holes, and I fell into the basement. As I fell, I noticed that the basement with the overhead wooden floorboards looked a lot like the concrete dividers in the ceiling of a parking garage. That's when I noticed a car. The back half of the car seemed to be filled with a thick dense black fog, if that makes sense. I couldn't see what was inside the backseat of the car."

As Carly recounts this, dread threatens her senses. "As I walked over to it, I felt overwhelming fear and I felt icky. I tried to see what was inside, but it felt like pure evil. I don't really know how to describe this. Right then, when I was trying to look inside the car, I woke up. I couldn't catch my breath. I was sweating and really scared."

"Icky? Why did you choose that word?"

"I dunno. That's how I felt."

"It just isn't a word that adults normally use. It is a word that a child might use."

"Does that mean something, that I would use a word a child would use?"

"Well...."

"Can't you just interpret my dream or something?"

"They're *your* nightmares. From all I've read and learned over my career, a lot of times nightmares are our mind trying to help us indirectly face and resolve the events of the day or unresolved feelings–things you're not ready to face head-on. There's no 'science' that addresses nightmares, because they're for the most part subjective."

"So, what you're saying is it's up to me to figure this out because this is my nightmare?"

"Well, I can guide you, but more or less, yes. How old are you in the dream?"

"Pretty young."

"Does the checkerboard floor seem familiar?"

Carly looks down, shaking her head, then nodding. Exhaustion creeps over her, wearing her down. "Yes. It reminds me of the house I grew up in. The basement too."

"I'd like to put you in a relaxed state again. I know you had a painful experience previously, but if this succeeds, I think this will allow you to sneak past your defense system. We're going to just focus on this nightmare. Is that okay?"

"I'm not so sure I want to after the last time." Carly sighs. After pausing, she says, "I guess I need to do *something*."

"This time, I want you to watch what's happening as if it's up on a screen. Essentially, this will remove you from directly experiencing this. Does this make sense?"

"I think so. You want me to imagine that I'm watching myself do what you ask me to do, rather than doing it myself."

"Exactly. Okay, sit back, and close your eyes. Just focus on your breathing, in and out, in and out, and relax."

Carly calms as Dr. Mentes continues speaking in a soft, soothing voice.

"Take deep, slow, calming breaths, in and out, in and out. Now relax, and imagine you're watching yourself walking down a hall and past doors with numbers on them."

Carly starts to tense, echoes of her last vision nag at her senses.

Dr. Mentes continues, "Remember, you are watching yourself. See the painted numbers, black on white doors or white numbers on black doors, whichever you like."

As Dr. Mentes continues the hypnosis, leading Carly to her dark and elusive memory, Carly's body tenses. She catches herself holding her breath. She breathes in deeply.

"Let me know you're still okay. Just nod, don't say anything, just focus on your breathing and relax. Remember, we can stop anytime. You're in control."

Carly nods, struggling with increasing trepidation, trying to calm herself.

"Continue watching yourself walk down the hall past the numbered doors–nine, eight, seven, six, five, four, three, two, then and at the end of this hallway, you see door number one. Observe yourself opening this door. As you open the door, watch yourself enter into the last scene in your dream from last night. Look around and see the floor and ceiling. Observe it is the parking garage from your dream. You see the car that was also in your dream. Watch yourself walk up to it."

Carly watches herself reach the car, and is overcome with fear. Her heart races, her breathing shallows. "I feel like I'm being pulled down, sinking into quicksand. I can't breathe."

"Carly, you're safe. Walk away from the car. Focus on your breathing, in and out. Pretend you're observing these events as if they were on a movie screen. Watch yourself as you walk up to the car. Remove yourself from the situation."

Carly nods once again. "Okay."

"Now imagine you see yourself on the screen walking up to the car. What do you see?"

Carly struggles to find words. In a voice that sounds like a little girl, she says, "It's all black. I'm scared."

"You're only looking at what's happening on the screen. You're not there by the car. You're safe. Can you see inside?"

"I don't think so, but I want to." Carly pauses. "I feel icky."

"Can you see past the darkness?"

"I don't wanna see. It's evil."

After momentarily pausing, Dr. Mentes says, “Okay, watch yourself back away from the car. Let’s get you back up the stairs.”

As Dr. Mentes proceeds through the process of bringing Carly out of the relaxed hypnotic state, Carly has a powerful sense of dismay that threatens to smother her like a pillow being held over her face.

“Now, whenever you like, gently open your eyes. When you do, you will feel calm and relaxed.” Dr. Mentes pauses to let Carly regain her present awareness. “How are you feeling?”

Staring at the ground, Carly says, “Okay, I guess. I couldn’t see past the darkness. Something bad was in there. I felt icky. It’s the only way I can describe it.”

“This was probably a memory from childhood. Like I mentioned before, *icky* is not a word that adults use. Was the icky feeling located on any certain part of your body or was it your entire body?”

Carly considers for a moment. “It was my lower, um…my bottom.” Filled with anguish, Carly shudders. “I’ve read a lot of those transcribed therapy sessions. It’s like I’m fitting together a puzzle, but there are still many pieces missing. Please outline why I was coming to see you. I think it may help me even if it hurts, I think it will help me know the bigger picture.”

“Well, you first started seeing me for marital difficulties. You’d told me you and your husband had grown apart. You had never connected with him emotionally or physically. It appeared you were just going through the motions of being married. You were depressed and angry. We were working on the reasons for your anger, which I believe stemmed from you systemically being abused–physically, mentally, verbally, and sexually–by your brother, your father, maybe your grandfather, and there's an abusive female figure in there somewhere too, but I was unable to identify who. I don't believe it was your mother, because she was absent working. Then she was very ill. Then, she died when you were very young.

"When you first came to see me, your daughter was about one and a half or two, which, as I understand it, is the age you were when you were first abused. I'm uncertain about the exact timeline.

"It was a year or so after you started therapy, that your little girl was found. Then your husband died a couple months later. Of course, these two new tragic events created new issues for you to resolve. You experienced so many negative events in your childhood. Most people don't even read about this type of thing, let alone have it actually happen to them."

Carly's chest tightens as she struggles to keep herself from crying. She looks toward the windows, hoping for some kind of distraction, but nothing draws her attention from Dr. Mentes' words.

"One thing I've seen is that you're very strong and determined and extremely resilient."

Carly chokes back tears.

"When you become overwhelmed with feelings, I would like you to sublimate those feelings into something else. For example, clean your kitchen, or parts of your kitchen, or try and write out your feelings in your journal. Also, I would like you to draw or paint your feelings to express these. Just isolate one feeling and pick a color and paint just that."

"Oh yeah, I forgot. I was trying to *draw* my feelings after I got home from Robert's house, like you suggested. I asked my inner little Carly how she felt, and I was trying to draw a picture of that. I started drawing what I hoped was a sad little girl, maybe with some tears in her eyes, but ended up with a little blond girl no more than four years old, covered in black-and-blue marks just wearing a pair of underpants. As I continued to draw, I felt the picture needed to be all black–the girl was overcome with overwhelming sadness. Tears became rage that covered the entire sheet. I ended up using a piece of charcoal, covering the entire page with intense black *X*'s, using so much force I shredded the sheet of paper."

"That sounds like deep sadness being covered up with a great deal of anger. When you go home, do some more work with that. Bring those pages back for the next visit. We can talk about them then."

Reluctantly, and with little hope for the days before her next visit, Carly says, "Okay."

She solemnly walks from Dr. Mentes' office with reality seeming closer and yet farther away at the same time. Her mind is temporarily numbed from all she just shared with Dr. Mentes.

The horror of the car resurfaces. Carly tries to shed it, to absorb any brightness she can to combat the darkness. One step at a time, she makes her way to the sidewalk.

Will my thoughts always be plagued with this darkness?

CHAPTER THIRTY-NINE

AWAKENING

On her way home, Carly mulls over Dr. Mentes' words–resilient and strong. *I certainly don't feel that way.* Carly's mind wanders. *I love the way Robert smells and how he makes me feel.*

That nightmare. I wonder what the blackness can be? What is it?

She breathes in the familiarity of her apartment upon opening the door. She puts on the blues–Muddy Waters. Tequila, lime, salt with a Xanax chaser–just what the doctor ordered...and a second, then a third shot.

What is that blackness? Carly tries to reach into the darkness and see what's there, drawing upon every ounce of her courage in the process. With paper on her tabletop and a charcoal pencil, she draws with her left hand, trying to engage the emotional side of her brain and her inner child to sketch what frightens her so. She goes through several pieces of paper until a pattern emerges into gray-black streaks.

She tries to distance herself from the image; awareness dawns–it's the design on a car seat, from which she can't back away.

Feeling something akin to a freight train hitting her, Carly suddenly recalls being pinned down in the back seat of a car. She looks down at her pretty, blue, frilly dress. She sees the black and gray design of the car seat as her face is being forcefully shoved into it. She senses the anger from whoever is holding her down–sodomizing her.

She feels icky.

Carly cries from deep within herself, a gut-wrenching sob as if her insides are being yanked out. She remembers, as a child, going into the bathroom afterward, touching her bottom. It's hot. It hurts. It's bloody. Deeply saddened and feeling newly bereft and betrayed at this realization, her mind spirals down a dark hole of despair.

She climbs up into her spot among the pillows, in the bay window, wrapping her arms around herself, and pats herself. *I'm here for you, little Carly. I'm so sorry, stupid, angry people did that to you. She hears Dr. Mentes' words, 'This is not happening now,' and is comforted.*

I'm going to protect you little Carly.

Carly sobs for a long time.

Without warning a floodgate opens. Many of her memories return. She pushes away the darkness as she remembers a lot about Robert. She remembers much of what they'd shared and how much she likes him. She remembers how he turns her on. She remembers the fun they've had together. *He was really patient with me and allowed me to get in touch with my sexual energy. Before him, I was afraid of that.* A strong rush of emotion and arousal and relief overwhelms her, and she feels as if she'll melt into a big puddle. *Awesome.*

As she sits there basking in those good feelings of all things Robert, a painful memory pierces her through: *Elizabeth.*

She walks over and looks at her picture, hugs it, and weeps again. *Oh, Elizabeth, I'm so sorry I wasn't there to protect you. I feel as if I'm losing you again.*

She also remembers her husband, Ben. *I wasn't just having problems with him. I didn't love him. I didn't have the feelings for him that I should have had, even though I cared about him. He was a wonderful man and father, but I was never physically or emotionally connected to him. Wow, why did I marry him? Because he loved me, even saying to me, "I wish you could see yourself the way I see you." At that point in my life, he was a good, logical choice. He was smart and funny and kind and honest and caring. I ran away from men that made me feel something emotional or physical. All those guys I never even got to know, because they tapped into my sexual energy. All of my feelings got repressed because of being molested and abused as a child.*

She remembers seeing Ben dead. She had come home from night class. Someone had telephoned the police because they'd heard a gunshot. He'd been in the shower, fully dressed, and blew the back of his head out. She was newly grieved to remember this. *How I failed you. I'm sorry for that. I'm sorry I didn't love you the way you loved me. You were in many ways one of the best parts of my life up to that point. You deserved more than I was able to give you.*

CHAPTER FORTY

ROBERT REMEMBERED

Carly listens to a few messages on her phone. Most of the recent communication is with Robert.

She considers calling him. She hesitates, even after his assurances. She remains unsure she has resolved the issues that caused her to abruptly run out on him during sex. *It's not Robert who caused that.*

Reaching past her anxiety, Carly takes a deep breath and dials his number.

"Carly!" Robert's voice explodes through the phone.

"Hi. How are you?"

"Doin' all right. Did you get my messages? Been concerned about you."

"I'm so sorry." Carly pauses. "I remember you. I remember us."

"What? How? That's great!"

"Parts of my memory returned. It's a long, unpleasant story, and I'll tell you about it another time. I'd like to get together and make amends for the other day. My place, I'll cook."

"Awesome! Tomorrow, 7:30? I'll be over after my karate class."

"Looking forward to this, more than you know."

"Me too. See ya tomorrow night."

***

Just breathe. I want everything to be perfect. Remember to breathe.

Carly cleans and straightens everything in anticipation of Robert's visit. When she ponders all that has gone on between them, excitement overtakes her. *Face still looks okay.* She laughs at herself. *Breathe.* She checks and rechecks in the mirror, changing outfits a couple times. First, shorts, then a dress, followed by a less formal dress and then a flowery print dress. She leaves her feet bare. *I don't want to mess this up.*

She changes back into jeans and a T-shirt while preparing dinner. *I want this to be special. This seems like a lot of work. I should've ordered delivery.*

She giggles. *What kind of music should I put on*? She searches for something soft and low key, selecting a Sarah McLachlan CD–*Fumbling Towards Ecstasy*. Carly sets the table, triple-checking the glasses for spots. She puts candles on the table and lightly sprays some perfume around the room.

"I'm so excited! I feel like my skin is the only thing holding me together," she says, peering into her fish tank. "Eddie, don't look at me like that." She continues talking to her fish and sprinkles some food in the tank. Eddie and the other fish devour the flakes. "See, it's just like that. When it's been a while."

She looks at the clock again. *I better get dressed.* As she changes back into her sundress, there's a knock at the door.

Breathless, she opens the door.

Robert stands there momentarily transfixed. "May I come in?"

"Sure, I'm just...I'm just...You're...."

Robert smiles. "You're breathtaking," he says, embracing her, lifting her off her feet.

Carly feels as if she's floating. Her reality is shaken. Desire weakens her. Her senses are lit up like fireworks exploding inside her. She relishes being in Robert's arms.

They just stand there in each other's arms for a while.

"I've missed you, m'lady." Robert kisses her deeply, sending a lightning bolt of exquisite pleasure through her with such force her knees threaten to give way.

"I missed you...I've...missed us," Carly breathlessly whispers in his ear.

They continue to luxuriate in their embrace, drinking in the pleasure.

"I'm glad you came back to me," Robert says, continuing to nuzzle her hair and neck. "So, you got your memories back?"

"An important one has–you." Carly smiles, looking deeply into Robert's eyes, and running her hands over his shoulders and down his arms. "I remember how much I like you. I love the way you pick me up off my feet and suck my bottom lip into your mouth when you kiss me. I feel like I'm floating when you do. I love the way you smell. I love the kind of man you are. I love the way you do art and the way you think," Carly gushes, overcome with a torrent of good feelings.

Robert smiles. "I'm glad." He glances around the apartment and toward the kitchen. "Yum, what smells so good?"

"I didn't remember if I knew how to cook, so I followed a recipe I found in the pantry," Carly says with a triumphant smile. "I'm baking lasagna."

"It smells awesome."

"Would you like something to drink? Wine?" Carly asks.

"Sure."

"Sounds good. I still need to put in the bread."

"Where are your wineglasses?"

"Haven't you been here before?"

"Remember, only the time I gave you a ride. You never let me know where you lived before."

"Oh, yeah. They're in the cupboard to the left of the sink." Carly shakes some garlic powder on the butter-covered bread.

Robert goes over to the sink, moves to the left, and opens a couple cupboards. He finds two wineglasses, then goes to the refrigerator and takes out the wine. "The corkscrew?"

"Drawer to the right of the sink."

Using the knife blade embedded in the corkscrew, Robert slices around the foil, peeling it back. A quick jab, followed by a couple quick twists, and the cork pops out. As he pours, he gestures to the table. "You already put glasses on the table."

Carly feels her face flush. "Oh, I forgot."

Laughing, Robert brings a glass of wine over to her.

Carly takes the glass with a smile and sips some wine.

"Wait." Robert puts a hand on Carly's hand holding the wineglass and looks into her eyes. "Here's to good times and many more meals, art, and nights and days of this, of us." Robert pulls Carly close and kisses her.

They drink.

Carly is soothed and exhilarated by both the wine and the intense connection she feels with Robert that lights up every cell in her body.

"So, where are your paintings?"

"Down the hall, the first door on the right is my studio, of sorts. I don't think I've done anything recently."

Robert walks down the hall and enters, stating, "This picture–it seems familiar."

The figure in the picture is nude, her head bowed, eyes downcast. Her right arm is up above her head at a right angle next to her face. There's a green-and-blue picture of the earth up in the top, left-hand corner, and the figure has a smiling mask that's peering up at the world. At the figure's core, is a black design of a sad-looking baby peeping out from between white swaddling wraps.

Carly walks back to see which painting he's talking about.

"What's this medium? Did you paint this?"

"It's a silk screen."

"A silk screen! I've always wanted to learn how to do that. How did you–this looks like it was painted. She *feels* so sad, but this has some amazing symbolism."

"I created the stencil by painting a negative image using wax and putting in a blocking layer, then removing the wax. It's a process that has a couple steps and multiple layers of inking. It sounds way more complicated than it really is. It's a self-portrait. The image at the center was a representation of my inner self or the wounded child part of me."

"That's so powerful. Masking all that pain, while smiling at the world. Love it!"

"I did that while I was doing some recovery work, so that was an expression of me at the time." Carly looks at the picture, connecting with some of the pain from her past. "Enough of this, let's have some fun."

"Yes, let's."

Robert moves over to Carly, takes one of her hands and starts to dance. He twirls her, and once he's behind her, he wraps his arms around her and kisses the back of her neck. "You move me." He unties the straps holding up her sundress and lets it drop to the floor. He takes her nipples between two fingers and begins to massage them while he continues kissing her neck.

Pleasure washes over Carly's body. She turns around and undoes Robert's shirt. As she pulls the shirt down around his shoulders, removing it, she notices some scars. She runs her fingers over them and kisses them. "I don't remember these."

Robert pushes her up against the door and moves her arms over her head, holding her hands up with one of his and grabbing a fist of her hair while pressing his full weight against her. He whispers in her ear, "I want you. I want to be inside you. I want you to come for me."

Weakened at this, she feels the heat from Robert's body, desiring to open herself to him completely.

Robert slips a hand down to her right nipple and pinches it.

Carly's body shudders and flushes crimson with desire.

He moves his hand down her side, caressing her, then sticks a finger up inside her. Her juices roll onto his fingers. He starts to massage her sweet spot.

Carly's sighs and moans, losing all sense of space and time as her breathing deepens.

Robert whispers, "I love to listen to you, to this. I love turning you on."

He picks her up and takes her into her bedroom, laying her on the bed.

Carly's head thuds into the headboard. "Ooh."

"Sorry."

The both smile.

Rubbing the bump, Carly shakes it off.

Robert undoes his belt.

The smoke alarm blares in the kitchen, a high-pitched and unwelcome chord breaks the mood.

Carly bolts up, throwing a spare T-shirt from a pile of laundry over her naked body, and runs into the kitchen, choking and coughing from the smoke. She flips on the overhead vent. “Well, that’s my offering to the food gods.”

“Who needs food anyhow?” Robert chuckles.

“We do. I’ll order some delivery. How does Chinese sound?”

“Just nectar of the gods and thee, ’tis all I need to sustain me.”

Carly chuckles, shaking her head. “I so wanted everything to be perfect!”

“Everything *is* perfect, now that you’re back,” Robert says, smiling, enveloping Carly in his arms.

Carly pulls out a menu and dials the restaurant. “What are you hungry for?”

“You.”

“Serious.”

“I *am* serious!”

As Carly orders, Robert starts kissing her on her neck and shoulders and caressing her nipples, playfully pinching them.

“Hi. I’d like to order some food for delivery. I’d like some cashew chicken,” she says, giggling, “an order of chicken fried rice, a couple of egg rolls.” Carly covers the receiver and turns towards Robert. “Anything else?”

“Told you what I wanted,” Robert whispers playfully.

"And an order of orange chicken. And could we get some extra, some extra...." Carly loses her train of thought. "Oh, sorry, soy sauce. About twenty minutes? Great!"

Carly giggles as Robert leads her back to the bedroom, all the while kissing her. "Do you remember me tying you up and blindfolding you?"

"Um, yes." Adrenaline shoots through Carly.

"Do you remember your safe word?"

Carly thinks a moment. "Ah...Rumpelstiltskin," she says, smiling and giggling with lust and rushing emotions. With her eyes locked with Robert's, Carly removes her T-shirt, and lies back in her bed.

Robert climbs up straddling her and whispers, "I want to try this. I'll go slow. Even though your memories are back, I don't want to rush this. You're safe. Let me know if it's too much." He takes one of the scarves wrapped around the headboard and ties it around one of Carly's wrists, then a second scarf for the other. Robert pulls up her right arm, kissing and caressing it. He ties the scarf around the post, pulling it snug. He kisses her neck, caressing her breasts and down her body. "You good?"

"Yeah." Carly's breathlessly responds as a flood of emotion pours over her.

He pulls up her left arm, kissing and caressing it, again tying the scarf around the post, pulling it snug. He grabs a third scarf, covering Carly's eyes, tying it behind her head.

The warmth and musky scent emanating from Robert's body as he moves on top of her are intoxicating.

As he kisses her neck, he whispers, "Is this what you want?"

Nodding, "Ye...yes, I do. I want this. I...." Overwhelmed with desire, Carly struggles to speak.

"Shh," Robert whispers. "You're mine."

She feels him trace down her jawline, her neck, continuing down her body. He pauses at her nipples. He takes each one in his mouth, licking and nipping them with his teeth.

Burning bright red, her arousal intensifies, like a lightning storm coursing through her. Weakened with desire, she moans. She breathlessly tries to make a sentence, "Rob...ert...I...."

"Shh. Quiet. Just enjoy this." Robert caresses her body. "You're beautiful, just breathtaking." He moves between Carly's legs, licking his way from her sweet spot, then back to her nipples, kissing, playfully pinching, and caressing her.

A knock rattles the door. Robert sighs, frustrated. "The food. That was fast. Don't move, I'll be right back."

Hearing Robert's footsteps down the hall, Carly breathes deeply. The ties around her wrist feel just tight enough. The thought that she's at his mercy sends shivers up her spine.

Her breathing settles, her heart with it. She tries to remain calm, awaiting his return with giddy anticipation.

CHAPTER FORTY-ONE

PROTECTOR
(30 MINUTES EARLIER)

Detective Daugherty glances up at Carly's apartment windows from his vantage point on the roof of the building across the street. He sees a black Honda approach, parking in an empty spot out front. He recognizes the car as belonging to Robert Hoy and is surprised at the pang of jealousy it triggers. He sighs, even more surprised at how long the feeling lingers.

He shakes his head, reminds himself why he's there. *I'm doing this for Carly. I have to protect her. I owe this to my sister.*

As he watches, he sees them cook and laugh and cuddle, all the things Daugherty had imagined doing with Carly. Jealousy stings him. Several times he closes his eyes and stops watching.

After they disappear from view. Daugherty considers, w*hat am I doing*? *Maybe this guy is safe enough. Maybe she's okay with him. They really seem to be into each other. It doesn't look like he wants to hurt her*. They haven't left, so they must still be in Carly's apartment. *Maybe I'll just go get something to eat.*

Daugherty heads to the gyro shop on the corner, the one with the window seat giving a clear view of Carly's apartment building.

CHAPTER FORTY-TWO

DINNER ARRIVES

Carly hears the familiar creak of the aged hinges, the expected sound as it closes. This is followed by a heavy thud.

"Robert?" she calls out. "Everything all right?"

Carly remains on the bed. Robert's ties bind her hands to the bedposts. An uneasy sensation seeps over her, with her nakedness heightening the feeling. She wiggles around, trying to loosen the binds.

No response, except the footsteps in the hallway, nearing her with an unfamiliar cadence. She senses someone in the bedroom doorway.

"Robert, was that our food?"

"Shh."

Carly's anxiety spikes. *This doesn't sound like Robert.*

After unzipping his pants, the man climbs atop the bed, then on top of her. He kisses her on her mouth and runs his hands down her body and caresses her breasts. He breathes out, "Shh."

The certainty that this isn't Robert crashes down on Carly like a tidal wave. "No! No!" Carly panics as memories of the night of her assault return. Carly violently struggles to break out of her restraints. She gets one hand free and violently thrashes about. She pulls off the blindfold. "You're the guy who…who…." Carly struggles to form a coherent thought, while being flooded with a barrage of emotions. "Stop!" she screams, kicking against the man's weight, trying desperately to struggle free.

"Yes! Please, fight me! Please!" her attacker says, breathing heavily.

CHAPTER FORTY-THREE

DET. DAUGHERTY

(FIVE MINUTES EARLIER)

After finishing his sandwich, Detective Daugherty starts to make his way back to the rooftop perch, he hears some chatter about Carly's address on the police radio.

"This is 20-William-12, we have a delivery driver, with a dark-blue jacket and blue jeans, approaching the building at 1452 West 18th Street. Looks like he's delivering Chinese food. License plate Foxtrot, Romeo, Yankee, Delta, 444."

The detective sees the delivery truck on the street and the driver enter the building.

Daugherty speaks into the walkie-talkie. "This is Daugherty. Can you see where the guy's going?"

"Yeah, it looks like the third floor. We don't have a good view of the hallway. The guy went up the elevator."

Something feels off. Just as he gets back to his original vantage point, he glances over at Carly's apartment and sees Robert fall to the floor by the front door, then watches a man walk toward the bedroom. "Damn." His adrenaline spikes.

"This is Detective Daugherty on stakeout at 1452 West 18th Street. All units in vicinity, I require immediate backup, apartment 303. I think our suspect just showed up."

Holding his breath, he races across the street, drawing his sidearm.

CHAPTER FORTY-FOUR

NICK OF TIME

Detective Daugherty opens Carly's apartment door, gun raised. Sirens blare in the distance, drawing closer. Scanning the apartment, he sees Robert lying unconscious on the kitchen floor.

Without checking on him, he rushes toward the sounds of struggle and screams from the bedroom down the hall.

He bursts through the bedroom door, sees a man on all fours over Carly, a beast looming over its prey. "New Brunswick PD! Get up! Now!"

The man backs off the bed, hands raised. He's wearing a jacket over a T-shirt, and the front of his pants are open.

Daugherty keeps his gun trained on the man. He's taller than Daugherty and bigger, more imposing.

Heart pounding, Daugherty draws the cuffs from his back pocket. "Turn around. Face the wall."

The man turns but whips back around, drawing a knife from the inner pocket of his jacket. Daugherty squeezes off a round. The window behind the man shatters. The man swings with an explosive force, slashing Daugherty's right arm, slamming him against the wall in the process.

Stunned, Daugherty drops his gun and staggers back against the doorframe.

The man pushes past Daugherty, disappearing into the hall.

Detective Daugherty struggles to reach his radio with his left hand. "This is Detective Daugherty at 1452 West 18th, Apt. 303. We need paramedics here now."

Despite the throbbing in his arm, he reaches across the bed, grabbing a throw to cover Carly. "Are you okay?"

***

Mortified and momentarily stunned, Carly nods, while loosening the scarf that binds her other hand. She pulls the cover up over herself. She looks Daugherty up and down, then focuses on his arm. "Detective! You're bleeding!"

"Just grazed my arm. I'll be all right. Are you okay?"

Shaken, Carly stammers, "I...where...where's Robert?"

"Unconscious in the kitchen. I called for paramedics."

"What?" Sighing, shaking her head, "I'm so embarrassed."

"I'm just glad I was in the neighborhood, so to speak."

"Were you watching me the whole time?"

"No. Which is why I didn't get here sooner. Your friend seemed safe enough, so I grabbed a sandwich from the gyro shop. I wanted to give you some privacy."

Carly takes a few deep breaths, then sits up. "I'm glad."

Daugherty winces. "I'll give you a minute. I'm gonna check on your friend."

***

Daugherty is halfway down the hallway when the paramedics arrive. They see Robert first, still lying on the kitchen floor, and start working on him. One wraps a blood-pressure cuff around his arm, while the other puts a clasp on his index finger. With some smelling salts, he rouses, slowly opening his eyes.

"Do you know what day it is, sir?"

"Saturday."

"And do you know where you are?"

Robert squints, "Um, I'm at my friend's apartment."

"Who's the mayor of New Brunswick?"

Robert laughs. "I wouldn't know that even if I hadn't been…whatever this was, out, unconscious."

"We need to take you to the hospital for observation."

"No, no, I'm good," Robert says, sitting up, rubbing his eyes.

The paramedic continues checking his eyes, shining a light in each. "Follow my finger."

The other paramedic states, "You really should come with us."

"No, I'm fine," Robert firmly states, shaking his head.

"Well, follow up with your doctor as soon as you can. If you have any signs of dizziness, blurry vision, confusion, nausea or headache, get to the emergency room. You really need someone to stay with you for at least 24 hours to keep you under observation."

"All right, thanks."

Detective Daugherty walks up and collapses into a chair at the kitchen table. "A little help over here, fellas?" Daugherty finally speaks up, somewhat disconcerted as the reality of the assault and the severity of his bleeding arm, forces itself into his awareness.

One paramedic rushes over and assists Daugherty with peeling off his jacket, revealing his bloody upper arm.

Trying to quell the exploding turbulence that lingers in the pit of his stomach, after the violent encounter with the assailant, Daugherty tries to focus on business, "Mr. Hoy, I'm Detective Daugherty, New Brunswick PD. What's the last thing you remember?"

Robert closes his eyes and covers his face with his hands. He takes in a deep breath and says, "Wow, I feel a bit woozy. I dunno, I'm kinda fuzzy. I was with Carly. We'd ordered some food, went into the bedroom. There was a knock at the door, I think. I don't remember much after that. What happened? Where's Carly?" He attempts to stand and wobbles feebly toward the rear of the apartment.

"Not so fast big guy." Daugherty holds up his hand, protectively blocking his movement.

Carly enters and rushes up to Robert, embracing him. "Are you okay?"

Robert responds. "Yeah, I guess. What happened?"

"Well, apparently, um...." Carly glances over at Daugherty.

Detective Daugherty states, "We had Carly under surveillance since before the time she went to the library. We figured our perp, who we believe was the one making the harassing calls, followed her from there and was just waiting for an opportunity. A plainclothes officer observed the scuffle with the delivery man and called it in. I'm guessing our perp was waiting by the elevator bank or something. I saw you drop from my vantage point from across the street and rushed in. I tried to apprehend the guy, but didn't have time to wait for backup since both you and Carly were in danger. We struggled, and the guy sliced my arm with a knife and got away, I'm guessing, down the fire escape."

"Thank you, Officer."

"It's *Detective*."

Robert glances at Carly. "Okay, you're coming with me to my place. You heard the paramedic. I shouldn't be alone right now, and neither should you."

"Your place it is." Carly replies with a demur smile.

Daugherty nods. “I agree. We’re going to keep watch on your apartment and you. I’ll call you tomorrow. We’ll need you to come down to the precinct in the next couple days to make an official statement.”

Robert responds, nodding, “Will do, Officer. Thank you again.”

CHAPTER FORTY-FIVE

DEBRIEFING

Jim arrives after Robert and Carly depart. "So, you think this was our guy?"

"I do."

"Walk me through what happened."

"Well, you know, I was keeping an eye on Carly."

Jim arches an eyebrow. "Uh-huh."

Daugherty recounts the events of the evening.

"You didn't wait for backup?" Jim shakes his head.

"There was no time. Ms. McCulley and Mr. Hoy were in immediate danger. I tried to apprehend the guy. We struggled, I got knifed, and he got away down the fire escape."

"Man." Detective Franklin continues shaking his head and running his fingers through his hair.

"I had to get in there and stop this guy," Daugherty protests.

"A couple of uniforms found the delivery driver unconscious in the back hall. Apparently, this assailant, who just maybe *is* The Tailor, used the food-delivery guise as a way to get in the door."

Daugherty nods with his head down.

"You could have been killed. You could have gotten *them* killed. We missed a great chance to get our guy. This is why we shouldn't take a personal interest in crime victims. It clouds judgment. That's why we have the rule about calling for backup."

"I know, I know." Detective Daugherty sighs, hanging his head. Knowing Jim is right, Daugherty still thinks he did the right thing. *Damn the torpedoes.*

CHAPTER FORTY-SIX

SAFE HAVEN

Once inside Robert's apartment, Robert and Carly stand in a long, healing embrace, neither saying a word.

Carly rests her head against Robert's chest. "That was awful. I mean, we were in the middle of something awesome, and that bastard showed up and could have hurt you. Ugh. I get sick just thinking of that guy's touch." She buries her face deeper. "I'm sorry. I'm going on about me. How are you feeling?"

"Well, I…I'm not sure. I'm really tired and don't feel like talking about any of this right now."

Carly nods. "Yeah, this was bad." She squeezes Robert.

"Please, make yourself at home," Robert says, giving Carly an extra hug. "I'll get some sheets for the couch."

"No, I can do that, just tell me where they are. I don't want to create any extra work for you."

"All of my sheets and stuff are right here," he says, gesturing to a bank of cabinets lining the wall adjacent the kitchen. "There are some blankets, and here are the towels and washcloths. Oh, just a sec." Robert walks up to his bedroom. "Here's an old football jersey you can wear to sleep in, until we can pick up some of your things."

Carly takes the well-worn, green-and-white jersey and turns it over. "Hoy" is inscribed on the back. Carly smiles.

"Make yourself at home."

Carly hugs Robert again. "Thank you, for everything."

She gathers up a set of light-blue sheets and a lightweight knit blanket. "Do you have an extra pillow?"

Robert thinks for a second. "You can use one of mine. I don't normally have guests." He walks up to the loft area once again and grabs one of the pillows. Carly follows him up the stairs. Robert turns and hands her the pillow. "Here you go."

Carly looks at the bed and reluctantly accepts the pillow. She smiles and considers suggesting sleeping together in the queen-sized bed, but thinks better of it. "Sleep well."

"I have to go into the city for work in the morning. I'll try not to wake you." Robert pauses. "I don't want you going back to your apartment alone. Either me or that cop should go with you."

"Okay." Carly gives Robert another hug, leans up and kisses him, then turns to walk down the stairs.

Robert pulls her close and gives her another all-encompassing hug.

She lights up at his touch. After, she walks down the short flight of stairs. Carly prepares the couch with the sheets. She moves a couple of the extra sofa pillows into a pile on the end table, stretches the fitted sheet out over the sofa cushions, lays out the flat sheet, and throws the blanket down. She folds the one corner up diagonally, making a picturesque sleeping spot.

Robert watches Carly from the landing. "Sweet dreams."

Carly looks up. "You too."

Robert turns, disappears, and the lights go out.

Carly slides in between the welcoming sheets that feel cool and crisp on her body. As she lays her head on the pillow, she breathes in deeply, enjoying Robert's musky scent. She snuggles into the couch and wraps herself in the sheets and blanket, feeling safe.

***

Carly struggles through a heavily wooded forest, the ground strewn with roots, leaves, and stones. She starts at a guttural noise. Sounds of a wild animal fill the air. Fear washes over her. Someone chases her, as if they're trying to kill her.

I have to get away.

The scene changes. Inside an old house, at night, Carly senses evil swirling around her. She tries to get away from something or someone. The threat of death remains.

The scene changes again. Carly lies in bed and sees the ethereal specter of a beautiful woman dressed in an alluring purple negligee, rise up from the end of the bed before she morphs into a deadly snake, striking at her belly with dangerous fanged jaws.

Carly drowns in adrenaline-soaked fear.

With a violent start, Carly wakes, breathless. Sweating and shaken, she sits up, pausing for a moment. *Just a nightmare.*

She tiptoes up to the loft and watches Robert, and for a short time listens to his deep, even breaths. She debates, then crawls under the covers next to him. She's comforted by the warmth and smell of his body.

Robert startles. "Wha...."

"I just had the most awful nightmare. Hold me."

"Sure." Robert pulls Carly to him and wraps his arms around her, kissing her on her forehead.

As Carly lays her head on Robert's chest, she can hear his heart beat. She feels safe and protected. *I wish I could feel like this all the time.* She breathes in deeply. *Robert smells so good. His skin feels amazing.*

Cradled in Robert's arms, she falls asleep.

CHAPTER FORTY-SEVEN

COMPLETELY SAFE

The telephone's harsh discordant ring awakens Carly, her arms still wrapped around Robert.

"Let the service get it," he says.

They look at each other and kiss.

"You're amazing."

Carly says, "I have morning breath, my hair is messy, and you're telling me I'm amazing?" Shaking her head, "No, *you* are amazing."

"This is good. We need much more of this." He starts to kiss and caress Carly, when the telephone rings again. "Oof." As he rolls over to look at his phone, he realizes what time it is. "Oh shit! I have a presentation. I should have been there already to get this going." He picks up the call. "Hi. Yeah, I realize. I'll be there shortly."

He turns to Carly, "Sorry to run out so fast, but I have to get to work. I have a presentation to the higher-ups."

"You move me. Before…last night, it was…amazing." She sighs with a dreamy smile.

"There will be much more of this. I'll be home later this afternoon. Call that police officer and make sure someone's here or outside while I'm at work."

"Can I make you some breakfast?"

"What? No," chuckling, "I'll get something on the way." Robert rushes around, freshens up, throws on a shirt and jeans and shoes, wets and combs his hair with his fingers. "I'll be back this afternoon."

Robert pauses to kiss Carly. "I have to run."

"Bye."

Carly goes back and lays down. She immerses herself in the smell of the sheets and covers, rolling into the warm spot where Robert was just lying as waves of pleasure course through her. She smiles thinking of Robert, his smell and the warmth of his skin. Her body starts to tingle and throb.

***

There's a knock at the door. Carly looks through the peephole. Upon seeing it's Detective Daugherty, she opens the door.

"Hi, Detective."

"John."

"You know, John, you saved me yesterday. Thank you for that. I think that makes you a hero. How's your arm?"

"More sore than usual, but I'll live. I'm going to keep an eye on you today."

"You're wounded. I thought you were going to send an officer to keep an eye on me. I don't want to be taking up so much of your time."

"I had the day off. A few days, actually, because of my arm, but I figure it's part of my public service–to protect and to serve, remember? As I said before, I take my oath very seriously."

Carly pleads, "I need to go to my apartment and get some things."

Detective Daugherty shakes his head. "That's not a good idea."

"You'll be there. Can't we make sure we aren't followed or anything like that? Do some cool spy maneuvers?"

"Spy maneuvers? You watch too much TV. Why don't you give me a list, and I'll go over and get the things you want. Our perp will be less likely to be looking for me. I'll be able to get in and out unnoticed, hopefully."

Carly considers this. "I don't know. I want my clothes, and I haven't found too many guys who can tell the difference between dark blue and navy, so I think we should go together, and we can be *vewy, vewy* quiet," Carly says in her best Elmer Fudd voice.

Reluctantly, Detective Daugherty agrees. "I guess, but I want you to wear a hat or hood or something to try and change your appearance a bit."

"A hood? I don't think so. I'll put on a baseball hat and braid my hair. That will change how I look."

Daugherty shakes his head. "Okay, but I really don't think this is a good idea."

Appreciative of the detective's concern, Carly works to convince herself that everything will be all right, that the unknown man who has been trying to hurt her, won't be lying in wait for her to return.

CHAPTER FORTY-EIGHT

WHAT COULD GO WRONG?

Carly pauses at the threshold of her apartment. The door stands open, yet she hesitates. She wonders, if this place will ever feel like home again.

She glances around, settles on the aquarium, something that has brought her a sense of normalcy, of routine. The filter murmurs as bubbles pour forth from the pump.

Daugherty hesitates behind her. "Everything all right?"

She nods. With a deep breath she steps inside. Carly shakes some ripe-smelling flakes of fish food from the yellow container. The pieces spread across the surface until some start sinking or are gobbled up by her fish. "Eddie, I'm going to be gone for a couple days. Don't worry, you guys will be fine."

She furtively looks down the hall toward her bedroom. The memory of her attacker's footsteps haunts her thoughts. Adrenaline surges through her as she is forced to relive last night's events.

All her stuff remains as she'd left it. Bedclothes a tussle, pillows stacked tight against the headboard. Noticing a piece of plywood the superintendent apparently affixed over the window, she pulls the shades closed.

She slides open the closet door, half expecting the attacker to be standing there. She stiffens, recalling the feel of his hands on her skin and the smell of his breath.

Inside, there's nothing but her clothes. She sighs with relief.

She grabs her suitcase and gathers some items. She looks at some of the pictures adorning her nightstand and vanity, reflecting on her newly found memories. As she turns over a picture, she remembers her husband and daughter. Sadness wells up inside. *I can't be dwelling on this now*. She puts down the picture with a sigh.

***

Carly closes her apartment door and steps into the hallway. She looks up into the detective's eyes. Her mind wanders back to Robert. She is momentarily flooded with pure delight and smiles. "Hey, I have a great idea, the fair is in town. You game?"

Daugherty says with a grin, "It could be fun, but I don't know."

"We could just go, try all the gross food, drink some beer, waste some money trying to win those silly prizes, get our palms read, see the animals. I think they have a great Rolling Stones cover band performing."

Daugherty hesitates, uncertain about being among so many people, out in the open. "I don't know if it's such a good idea."

Carly shakes her head. “No, I think it’s just what I need to take my mind off all this stuff. It’ll be fun.”

Carly follows Daugherty down the hall, half running to keep pace with his long strides.

He states, “I haven’t been to a fair in years.”

“That’s one of the great things about fairs, at least this one. They rarely change. You can always count on the grilled corn, cotton candy, and whatever outlandish food they’ve thought to deep-fry.”

Carly breathes in, imagining the sweet aroma and char of the grilled corn. Her mind drifts back to her childhood. She fondly recalls her yearly summer trek to the county fair, where she would dream of owning a horse. With a quick refocus, Carly returns to the present, steps into Daugherty’s car, and watches the streets pass, the people fly by, the world a blur, matching her thoughts.

CHAPTER FORTY-NINE

THE FAIR

The enticing smells of popcorn and cotton candy lure Carly as she opens the car door and steps onto the matted grass-and-dirt parking lot. Colorful carny booths, food vendors, and brightly colored rides beckon along the main thoroughfare.

A wellspring of joy surges through her, bringing a delight from childhood, a brief respite from the horrors of her past and the uncertainty of the present. "I love playing these games. I want to go see the horses and ride the Ferris wheel."

"Are you hungry? How about a beer?" Daugherty asks.

"Sure, yeah. Beer, food. I love the barbecue at the fair. I want to do everything."

"So, you remember going to fairs?" Daugherty asks with a smile.

"Why yes. I hadn't realized that, but I remember going during the summer every year with friends. Being here makes me feel like a kid again," Carly responds smiling.

"This is good. Follow me."

Carly follows Detective Daugherty over to the beer garden where they get their IDs checked and receive wristbands. Carly flinches, remembering the ties Robert secured to her wrists that left her at the mercy of her stalker.

"What do you have on tap?"

"Only Budweiser, sir."

"Okay, two Buds then."

Carly, all aflutter from the colorful sights and sounds, says, "Come on, I want to go play. Let's go over here and try this game."

They walk up to a wood-framed booth painted in vibrant blues, yellows, and reds. Painted bears dance along walls lined with stuffed animals, all waiting for winners to take them away.

"How much to play?" Carly gushes.

"Two dollars, ma'am," responds the thin carny.

"How do you play?"

The man behind the counter, who doesn't appear to have bathed in weeks, is dressed in an old plaid shirt and torn jeans. "See this here red circle? Ya just cover it up with these three blue disks."

Carly watches the man effortlessly perform the task and cover up the red circle with the disks.

"That looks easy." She exchanges her two dollars for the three disks. Concentrating, she lays them down one by one and all but covers the red circle. "Aw."

"That was really close, ma'am. You wanna try a'gin?"

"Can I see you do that again?"

The man adeptly covers the circle with the three disks.

"Wanna go a'gin, ma'am?"

"Sure."

Carly tries again, unsuccessfully.

"Ya 'most had it that time, ma'am. Wanna try one more time?"

"No, thanks," she says.

The pair continue making their way down the main fair walkway.

"You know, there's probably a magnet under the table that they push to stop you from placing the disks," Daugherty says.

It's like life: maybe not always fair, maybe things don't always go your way, but you still participate.

"I know these games are rigged, but it's still fun to try." Carly keeps walking, excitedly looking at all the sights. She spies the cotton-candy maker. Rushing up, she begs, "Can I have one of those, please?"

"Sure, that'll be seven dollars."

"Do you want some?"

"No, thanks, too much sugar for me."

Carly hands the guy a ten-dollar bill. "Just one, please."

She stares fascinated as the man plies his craft and builds a huge mound of cotton candy around a paper cone. He hands Carly her treat.

"Thank you." Smiling, Carly says, "I love this."

As they continue walking, Carly sees a shooting-gallery booth. "Are you a good shot?" She poses the question to Detective Daugherty.

"I'm fair."

They walk over to the shooting gallery.

"How many targets do you need to hit to get that stuffed bunny?" Carly asks the scruffy-looking attendant.

"Well, ya hit three of these in any round, and ya git a prize, then ya trade up."

Detective Daugherty picks up one of the rifles and looks down its barrel through the sight, then each of the other four that lay on the table. "I actually got a badge for this when I was in Boy Scouts. How much to play?"

"Five dollars, sir."

"Okay, I'll try." Detective Daugherty hands the man a five-dollar bill. "I'm going to win one of these stuffed bunny rabbits for you. He has such a cute face." Detective Daugherty takes aim and hits four of the five targets that pop up.

"Here's a winner!" The man hands Detective Daugherty a tiny plastic toy.

"Wait, you said we win if we hit three targets, and I hit four."

"Yes, sir. Ya won, and ya got dat prize. Ya have to trade up."

"How many of these do I have to win, or how many trades are there?"

"Well, ya trade up to this," the man holds up a series of bigger and bigger stuffed toys, "'til ya git to this-un."

"Okay, game on. I want to go again."

Carly smiles. "I need to find the little girls' room. Don't worry, I'll be right back. Besides, there are hundreds of people around, and it's just right over there. I'll be fine."

Detective Daugherty reluctantly agrees, glancing toward the restroom area. "Okay." He continues shooting, somewhat distracted by the ego-challenging quarry, hitting most of the targets each time.

Carly weaves her way through the crowd, sees the shack with the restroom signs hanging over two separate entrances. She glances around. People come and go, strolling by, some too close with the press of the crowd, others peering with vacant stares in their enchantment of the fair.

She senses someone following close behind with heavy steps. Glancing to her right, she tries to catch a glimpse from her periphery but doesn't make out anything or anyone. She breathes a sigh of relief and steps toward the door of the women's room.

Someone's hand comes up in front of Carly's face from behind, covering her mouth and nose with a liquid-soaked cloth. Everything falls to darkness.

CHAPTER FIFTY

THE RECKONING

Carly startles awake. *Where am I*? She tries to move one of her arms. *Ugh*. Sensing she's gagged, facedown, naked, her knees up underneath her, her arms stretched out above her and tied to posts. She's sickened upon realizing she's being savagely fucked from behind. The man stops thrusting and climbs off. Waves of adrenaline-fueled rage mount in intensity inside of her, threatening to drown her. Attempting to speak, "Wha…? Who are…you?"

"Shut up, you stupid bitch. The gag is to keep you quiet." The man hits Carly with some type of board, knocking her sideways. Stunned, Carly sees stars, her ears ring. As she turns her head, she can see him–in his fifties, white, with thinning, greasy, gray hair and glasses. As he gets up off her, he hoists his zipper up on his dirty work trousers and tries to tuck in his shirt, showcasing his potbelly.

Scowling at her, the man snaps his fingers. "Get with the program, bitch. You're mine now, and there's nothing you can do about it. I'm not done with you."

A sharp pain pierces Carly's neck. She moves around, attempting to alleviate the ache, but her movements are slow and muted.

As best she can tell, they're in what appears to be the upper floor of an old, abandoned building. The rusted walls are populated with broken windows, sporting cracked panes of glass, couched between intermittent paneling falling off, sorely in need of repair.

A pallid stench, a combination of rotten vegetables and urine, invades Carly's senses. Muffled by the gag that has loosened slightly, Carly tries to speak. "Why are you…?"

The man, ignoring her, climbs on top of her and unties one of her arms. "You're getting what's coming to you. Your type thinks you can get away with anything you want."

Carly writhes around and yelps, "Le...me...go."

"Shut up. I don't wanna listen to your voice, bitch." He slams Carly in the head with his fist. Then harshly grabbing her lower face with his right hand, he scowls right up close to her face. "Right now, I'm calling the shots. We're going to party some more." He unties her other arm, turns her over, then reties both arms. The man starts to run his hands up and down Carly's body. "You have such nice tits and such a fresh, young body. Just like a little girl." After the man grabs one of her breasts, he climbs off the mattress, undoes his sagging trousers, then moves toward her, intent on shoving Carly's legs up, positioning himself to fuck her again.

Carly violently struggles with renewed vigor, attempting to get this beast off her. She loosens one of the ties around her right hand, but her movement is muted. She feels as if she's trying to move in quicksand.

The man spits out at her. "Please struggle. Better than ya just lying there like some cold fish."

As adrenaline and anger spike inside her, Carly tries to kick the man sideways, kneeing him in his crotch, drawing a groan of pain that stretches out into a predatory growl.

The man strikes her with the back of his hand. Carly reels, her head spins. She sees stars. The world around her blurs, then fades once again to darkness.

She rouses once more. Just as the man begins to thrust inside her, Carly hears, "Police! Stop what you're doing, and move away from the girl." *Detective Daugherty.*

The man grunts looking up, and turns toward Daugherty. He holds up his right hand in a *stop* motion. "Fuck. You've got this all wrong. Me and my girl are just having some fun."

Carly struggles and yelps, trying to call to Detective Daugherty. Shaking her head she tries to yell, "Help...me!"

"Just like you were doing in her apartment the other night? Get off the girl, now! Stop what you're doing, and get up, hands up."

As the man moves to stand, he quickly reaches under the mattress and pulls out a large hunting knife, brutally thrusting it under Carly's neck. "Drop the gun or I'll do her."

Detective Daugherty fires off a round from his gun as a warning shot. "I said drop it! Now!"

While the man's attention is momentarily diverted, Carly twists, kneeing the knife away from the man, and with her newly freed hand adeptly grabs it and violently rams it into the side of his neck, twisting it, with a rage-filled malice, growling as she does.

The man slumps to the side, away from Carly. Blood pumps from the wound, pooling across the mattress and down onto the floor. Solemnly, Carly observes it with a dead stare, unable to look away.

Daugherty rushes over and checks to see if the man still has a pulse. He covers Carly with his jacket.

As Carly is jolted to her core, memories begin to flood back. Awareness emerges like a snake suddenly striking out of tall grass. She sickens as she realizes this is the man who beat her up and attacked her and Robert at her apartment.

Carly remembers.

She remembers The Tailor, how she got into the situation where she was beaten. She remembers the man in front of her and how she first came into contact with him.

A deluge of memories pours into her mind. Images flash. She recalls smells, touches, sounds, each providing a rush of recollection, a terrible surge of sensation.

Dizzy, she experiences a new, unsettled awareness. Rage surges inside her.

Other police officers arrive.

"A little help here," Daugherty says.

Another police officer rushes over, checks on the man.

Detective Daugherty gently pats Carly on her back. "You're okay. We got him."

CHAPTER FIFTY-ONE

CLEANUP

"Get this piece of–," Detective Daugherty clears his throat, "guy out of here. Put this knife into evidence. We do this by the book." He points out the blade to the attending tech, now hovering around and taking pictures. The click of the camera's shutter is but one sound among the cacophony of noise resounding through the crime scene.

The tech pauses his grim photography to take the knife. "We got it, Detective. By the book."

The attention that is sure to accompany this case warrants extra care and caution, even above Daugherty's high standards. "I just want to make sure."

"We know, sir."

Detective Daugherty walks over to Carly who is now sitting on a gurney by the ambulance. "Wow, I feel woozy." She sighs, shaking her head. "I need to...clean...get this filth off me. I need a bath."

"We need to do a rape kit."

"I don't want to go to the hospital again. I'm okay."

"There's more to it than that," Detective Daugherty adds. "You need to be thoroughly checked out. We need to talk to you about what happened, take your official statement. Given your past with this creep, it wouldn't hurt to see a social worker."

Carly bows her head as tears wet her cheeks.

"It's over. You're okay," Daugherty states, attempting to comfort her.

Walking back over to the mattress stained with the man's blood, Detective Daugherty gestures to the tech taking photos. "Make sure you get pictures of this from all angles."

Daugherty grimaces and shakes his head, looking down at the blood-stained mattress.

The other officer continues. "So, this is our serial killer, The Tailor? The guy Detective Franklin's been looking for?"

"Not a hundred percent sure, but we think this is the guy who has been harassing Ms. McCulley ever since she got away from him. He was trying to finish his kill."

"I thought this Tailor only took out child abusers?"

Daugherty scowls, shaking his head. "Um, I'm not certain. Jim's the person to answer that. It appears that way based on the cases which we are currently aware, grouped together by commonality. This may be…oh, who knows? Let's not get off on some speculative tangent."

"I've been following this case," the eager young officer says, a little too enthusiastically for the circumstances. "I want to be a homicide investigator."

"Well, wherever this guy got his information, he must have gotten his wires crossed." Daugherty pauses, then says, "If this was The Tailor, her husband abused their little girl, not her."

***

Carly glances up at Daugherty speaking with the young officer, overhearing Daugherty's comment. *Her husband abused their little girl, not her.*

Officer Smith walks over, climbs up into the back of the ambulance where Carly is sitting, and asks, "How are you doing, miss? Do you feel up to answering some questions?"

Reluctantly, Carly nods.

"Do you remember how you got here? What's the last thing you recall?"

"Not much. It's all really kinda fuzzy."

A paramedic interrupts. "We need to get going. You can talk to her at Good Sam." Turning to Carly, he instructs, "I need you to lie down here for the ride."

Carly lies back on the gurney as the paramedic attempts to strap her in for the ride. "Can you just let me lie here? I promise I won't fall out."

The paramedic obliges, but covers her in a blanket, which he tucks in under her at various spots.

The world speeds past. The sirens blare, and the horns honk a few times while the ambulance moves out onto the street. Carly breathes in deeply, trying to calm herself. She struggles to keep it together. She shudders, recalling the events since she regained consciousness–the reek of the man's sweat, his guttural breaths, the detective's shot ringing in her ears, shoving the knife into the man's neck, then his blood pumping out in a wide arc, the exhalation of his final breath, and the knife clattering to the floor.

Carly replays comments she'd overheard from Detective Daugherty, which stung, if they were true. Her husband abused their daughter? The thought brings a fresh wave of raw anger and revulsion.

Upon arrival at the hospital, Carly is rolled into the emergency room. Various nurses and doctors flit around her, each performing their assigned tasks for incoming trauma patients. A young, clean-cut doctor examines her, patches up her cuts, and orders a CT scan. Soon after, a nurse completes a rape kit, collecting hairs and scrapings from under Carly's fingernails, performing a pelvic exam and placing all the related materials in tubes, on slides or in circular plastic cases for further examination. As Carly endures this, her mind is numb. She stares off into space as if she's not really there.

***

A woman approaches, her gait casual and relaxed compared to the hustle of the medical team. "Hi, Carly, my name's Melissa. I'm the staff social worker on call this evening. How are you feeling?"

"Numb. I just feel…I don't feel anything. I need a bath."

Carly glances down the line of beds in the ER and sees Detective Daugherty striding her way.

Carly says, "Thank you, Melissa, but do you mind if we continue in a few minutes?"

"No, not at all," Melissa says, noticing Daugherty approach Carly's bed. She departs.

Carly manages a weak smile. “Thank you again, Detective. That’s the second time you came to my rescue.”

“It’s what I do,” he says, smiling. “How are you doing? How are you feeling?”

“Okay. I don’t know. I think I’m okay. I’m...I don’t know. How did you find me?”

“I put a tracking device in your purse,” he says with a subdued grin, shaking his head. “Because of the interference with the power lines, it took more time to find you than I would have liked.”

“I have a question.” Carly inhales, hesitant to broach this subject. “I heard you say something to one of the other officers back there about my husband.”

“Oh?”

“You two were talking about The Tailor, and the officer said he thought The Tailor only targeted child abusers. You said the guy got it wrong, that it wasn’t me, that it was my husband. What exactly were you talking about?”

Detective Daugherty bows his head, purses his lips and sighs. His shoulders slump. He shakes his head. “I’m sorry you heard that. I know you’re not a child abuser.”

“Right, I didn’t abuse my daughter; I would never. I would have died for her.”

“I know. When I was investigating your assault, I pulled all the files we had on you, which included information about your husband and daughter.”

“Okay. So, tell me. How bad can it be?”

"Well, there's something about your husband's suicide that was never released publicly: he left a suicide note."

"What?"

"Some things might be better left alone."

"No. I need to know."

"I don't remember it down to the letter. Let's wait until you come down to the station, and I'll show it to you. Until then, let's just focus on getting you checked out and making sure you're okay."

Carly sighs, nodding. Breaking into a sweat, she feels the warmth of the room constricting her, closing in. She ponders if this is the answer that has eluded her, that her lost memories couldn't reveal.

"So, how's our girl?" Detective Daugherty asks one of the doctors hovering around Carly, hoping for some positive news.

"She appears to be okay. Other than the sexual assault, which we should by no means minimize, she has some muscle strain from being tied up, maybe a neck strain, some minor cuts and contusions on her face. Other than a possible mild concussion, she doesn't seem to have any residual effects from whatever it was that knocked her out. I will know more when I get the test results back."

Daugherty turns from the doctor, who has already moved on to the next patient. "What's the last thing you remember prior to waking up in that warehouse?"

"Um…we were at the fair. I remember getting the cotton candy, but after that, it's blurry to me."

"He must have grabbed you in the restroom."

"How did he find us?"

"I feel like this is my fault. He must have been watching your apartment. That's why I didn't want to go there."

"But I insisted." Carly states, shaking her head.

"I should've been more attentive, rather than let that carnival game occupy me. I could've at least been closer, maybe stopped him from taking you to the warehouse."

"I'm not blaming you," Carly says, managing a weak smile.

"It doesn't sound like you'll need to stay overnight. When you're discharged, and if you're up to it, I'd like you to come down to the station to fill out some paperwork, answer a few questions, and take a look at a few photos to confirm a thing or two about The Tailor."

"Deal," says Carly, suddenly overcome by overwhelming trepidation that seeps into her mind like an ominous cloud bank that precedes a violent storm. Carly shakes her head, looking past Daugherty to the ER entrance, where the lights of an ambulance flash in a steady metronomic beat.

"Whatever you're feeling, it's okay, it's normal. I have quite a bit of experience with trauma victims. Like I said before, it's gonna take time to get over all this, just give yourself that time. Nothing to be afraid of now."

"I'm not afraid, I'm…." Carly states defiantly, then pauses, reflecting on an ever-increasing anxiety.

She watches Daugherty walk toward the main ER desk near the entry.

I need a bath. I need to clean this disgusting stench off me.

CHAPTER FIFTY-TWO

RETURN TO THE POLICE STATION

Detective Daugherty parks in the special parking area for police officers, adjacent to the station. He steps from his car, moves around the front, and opens the door for Carly.

They walk up to the now-familiar six-story brick building and into the room where Detective Franklin is waiting. Jim stands to greet Carly. "Please, have a seat. Can I get you some coffee, water, a soda, anything?"

"Nothing, thanks."

"How are you feeling?"

"Um, I dunno. Something like this makes me appreciate life," she says, shaking her head. "This all happened so fast, I'm not sure how I feel. I'm just glad it's over."

"Okay, then let's get right to it. You understand why we asked you to come here, right?"

"Um, yes. I think you want my take on the events from the last couple days."

"Precisely." Detective Franklin confirms.

"We were at the fair," Carly says, gesturing toward Detective Daugherty. "He was looking after me while my friend Robert went to the city for work. Neither of them wanted me to be alone after that guy attacked me at my apartment."

"We'll get to that in a minute. So, what's the last thing you remember prior to waking up in that warehouse?"

Clearing her throat and sitting more upright, Carly responds, "I'd gotten some cotton candy, and I think I went to the restroom. I don't remember much after that," she says shaking her head.

"That's where he must have grabbed you," says Jim. "In the restroom. How do you think he found you?"

Detective Daugherty interjects. "I feel like this is my fault. He could have been watching her apartment." Looking at Jim, he states, "We went back to her apartment to pick up some of her clothes."

"You two went to her apartment after the first attack? *Back* to her apartment!" Jim looks incredulous while writing everything down, shaking his head.

"Detective Daugherty saved me. Write that down too." Carly emphatically states, pointing her finger at Jim's notepad.

Continuing to shake his head, Jim, his lips pursed, gives a dissatisfied glance at Detective Daugherty.

"I had to pick up my things. I really couldn't trust anyone else to do that. I insisted."

"Okay, let's go back to the incident at your apartment."

"I'd asked Robert over to my place and was cooking dinner for him. We were fooling around, and the dinner I was cooking burned, so I ordered delivery. When the delivery man came with the food, I…I guess this guy had been watching my building and took the driver's place somehow. He knocked Robert out, then he came into my bedroom and started coming after me."

"Did you see the man come into your apartment?"

"No. Luckily, Detective Daugherty got there and saved me."

"Did you see the struggle between the man and Detective Daugherty?"

"Yes. They fought. Detective Daugherty had his gun on the man, and told him to get off me. Detective Daugherty attempted to handcuff him, but he swirled around and threw the detective against the wall, knocking him over and slashed his arm with a knife, I think."

Detective Daugherty and Detective Franklin exchange glances.

"Okay." Detective Franklin continues writing. "Then what?"

"The man ran out of the apartment and got away."

"After that, what did you do?"

"I got dressed and went to check on Robert. The emergency techs were there."

"Wait, you got dressed? You mean you were undressed?"

Shaking her head, Carly blushes. "Robert and I were fooling around before–."

Detective Franklin holds up his hand. "Okay, I get the picture." Hanging his head, rubbing the bridge of his nose, he squints and shakes his head again. He sighs and continues to write out the details. “After you went to check on Robert, what happened?”

“After the medics left, I went over to Robert’s loft and was there overnight. He had to go to the city for work and I called Detective Daugherty, who came to watch over me. I talked him into going over to my apartment to pick up my clothes and toiletries and stuff, then we went to the fair. Next thing I remember I woke up with that monster going at me doggy style.” Carly closes her eyes as a fresh wave of disgust courses through her.

“I’m sorry to make you relive this. What happened next?”

“He got off me and hit me a few times with a board or something. I tried to talk but was gagged. He kept yelling at me to shut up.”

“Did he say anything to you?”

“He said I deserved this and referred to me as one of *those* people.”

“Did anything else happen?”

“He flipped me over, untied one of my hands, and climbed over me getting ready to....” Bile rises in Carly’s throat, remembering the guy’s body odor and cheap cologne. She bows her head and covers her face with her hands. *I really need a bath.* “It was awful. Then I heard Detective Daugherty yell ‘Police’ and tell the guy to stop.”

Jim looks at Detective Daugherty.

Detective Daugherty nods.

"All I kept thinking was I didn't want to die. I'm not done yet."

"Okay, what happened next?"

"Detective Daugherty yelled at the man to stop what he was doing and get off me. The guy held up his hands, but then like lightening reached down pulled up a knife and held it under my throat. He yelled he would cut my throat if the detective didn't drop his gun. Detective Daugherty fired a warning shot. That's when I twisted, kneed the guy, grabbed the knife and stuck it into the side of his neck with all the force I could. It's kind of a blur. He slumped over and fell off me." Carly is stricken with the image of him lying there with a fountain of blood pumping out of his neck. "Then the officers and Detective Daugherty came over and finished untying me." Recounting all this, triggers a torrent of unwelcome emotions from shame to utter disgust. With her head down she takes in a deep breath. Anger and sadness well up as tears sting her eyes.

Detective Daugherty points out, "It was a knife that appears to match the murder weapon in the other Tailor killings."

"I'm sorry to be digging all this up again, Detective Franklin says. You've been through quite an ordeal. Thank you for your cooperation. Here's the name of our social worker." Detective Jim hands Carly a business card. "This is part of our outreach program to help victims of violence. There's no cost to you. She can help you deal with this."

Franklin nods, leaves, the door clicking shut behind him.

Carly turns to Detective Daugherty. "Tell me what you know about my husband."

Detective Daugherty asks, "Are you sure? Some things might be better left unknown."

"I appreciate your concern, but I feel like this may be another step in me regaining my memories."

"Okay, let me go get the file. I'll be right back."

After Detective Daugherty leaves the conference room, Carly walks back over to the war room dedicated to The Tailor. She circles the room, pausing in front of each grouping of The Tailor's victims. She studies the pictures, running her fingers across the images.

Detective Daugherty comes to the door. "Are you okay? We got him. There's nothing to be afraid of any longer."

Carly shakes her head. She turns and smiles. "I'm…I'm…."

"I have the file about your husband's suicide. Let's go back over to the conference room."

They walk back to the conference room as Daugherty rifles through the papers in the folder. "Let me see, here it is. You asked me earlier what I was talking about when I was speaking to the young officer at the warehouse. He'd mentioned that he was following this case. He asked how you fit into this, because The Tailor's victims have one primary thing in common, other than how they were killed."

"And that's what, exactly?"

"Some went to trial, some were convicted, but *all of them were accused* of violently abusing, molesting, and killing children in horrendous ways."

"What does this have to do with my husband?"

"He left a suicide note. This wasn't released to the press. I think it may have been buried in the file on purpose."

Carly blinks in disbelief. "Are you sure? Can I see that?"

I have to end my pain.
I cannot live with this anymore.
I raped and killed my daughter.
I'm an awful person.

"Yes. Maybe this was lost in the file by accident, or maybe the officer in charge did it out of compassion for you. You finding this out would not take away the loss or any of your pain. It would only add to your grief."

Carly sits, shell-shocked, staring at the note. "Wow, well, that's...this is a lot to take in. I have to...I need to go now. Thank you again for everything."

Carly exits the room. She doesn't look back or say another word.

EPILOGUE

The Tailor glares at the man tied up on a table in a shabby, broken-down room at an abandoned fleabag motel. Zip ties reinforced with duct tape bind him to a tabletop. Peeling and stained wallpaper covers the walls. A threadbare, faded area rug conceals the rotting timbers of the floor. The curtains dangle, broken away from the rusted rod above the window. There is no air conditioning. Through the open window, the acrid smell of urine wafts in, along with the rancid smells of garbage and sweat.

The man rolls his head. His eyelids flutter, then snap open. He struggles for breath against the duct tape over his mouth.

The Tailor rips it off.

The man gasps.

"Welcome back," the killer says.

The man–white, early fifties, a paunch around his midsection clinging to former hints of athleticism, struggles to break free. His cheap blue paisley tie and light-blue dress shirt, bearing a stain from a drip of morning coffee, lay in a pile next to him, along with his suit jacket and pants.

"You're not going anywhere. I learned my lesson last time. I had a guy tied up, and he got loose and turned the tables on me and could have killed me. I've taken extra precautions."

Terrified, the man struggles to speak. "Where…how did I…?"

"Where? You're in a godforsaken shithole motel. I used a rare herb in your drink that causes temporary unconsciousness. It quickly dissipates from the body and is virtually untraceable, unless someone specifically looks for it."

The man remains silent, then strains at his bonds.

"They nearly caught me, you know. Because of my MO." The Tailor drones on. "I removed the parts of the body that were involved in their crimes. I gouged out their eyes they used to covet their victims," the killer continues with an unsettling smile. "I cut off their feet they used to chase after their victims. I sawed off their hands that carried out their abuse. I cut off dicks, I sewed up vaginas–anything to prevent them from *ever* having any more kids to abuse," the killer snarls, slinking behind the man's back, like a lion stalking its prey before pouncing.

"Now, I'll have to change things up a bit. I haven't decided what I'm going to do with you yet, but don't worry. I'll make your body disappear after I'm done," The Tailor coos in his ear.

"But…why…?"

"Why? Thank you for asking." The killer leans over him looking him dead in the eye. "Because you're a violent child molester and abuser."

Terror flashes across the man's face. The Tailor stabs a finger in the middle of the man's forehead. "You brutally berated, beat, and molested Melanie, Eric and Chloe, your three stepchildren, over the course of two years, finally viciously killing them. You're the worst kind of human being," the killer continues, seething with rage. "When you should have protected these precious children, you instead took advantage of their innocence and trust in you. Your six-year-old stepdaughter, Melanie, should have been able to learn to love and trust–but instead, you beat her, sodomized her, raped her, and killed her. You systematically destroyed that little girl's life. Do you have anything to say for yourself?"

The man stares ahead in defiance.

"See this picture?" The killer waves a picture of a smiling young girl in front of his face. "Admit what you did!"

The man lays there in silence, with an insolent grimace on his face.

"ADMIT WHAT YOU DID!" The Tailor roars in the man's face, losing patience with his silence.

"She asked for it!" The man impotently protests. "She *wanted* it. She continually told me she loved me and wanted to marry me. She was all over me, hugging me and kissing me all the time–."

The Tailor spits back at the molester lying on the table, "No, she didn't ask for it. Little girls and little boys have to learn how to love with their opposite-sex parent. No one wants to talk about this, and because no one wants to talk about this, no one ever learns. Just because you feel aroused doesn't mean you act on those feelings. There's no possibility of mutual consent for sex between an adult and a child. Children are attempting to learn to love in its purest sense. They learn to be accepted and appreciated and loved. They learn to trust. It doesn't mean they're trying to seduce you to get you to have sex with them. Many men don't get this, don't think about this, or they don't care. They think that if they feel it, it must be true, without any consideration or thought to what their actions will cause or reap. Maybe they even think the child won't remember it, if they do it early enough, if they think about it at all.

"Society is partly to blame. They let companies peddle everything by stuffing sex down everyone's throat from an early age. No wonder men are so sexually charged and objectify women and girls as instruments of their own selfish gratification."

Scowling, the man on the table spits out a pall of air.

"You asked me before why I'm doing this. I *am* doing this for your stepchildren, the ones you should have protected. I was initially trying to find out who raped and murdered my little girl. It turned out, I married him. My therapist once told me, we're drawn to the same types of people who were part of our initial upbringing because unconsciously they feel comfortable to us. The real answer to your question–," the Tailor pauses and takes a deep breath, "I'm doing this because *someone* has to take out the fucking trash!"

After retaping the man's mouth shut, Carly starts her band saw.

AFTERWORD

This book does not condone nor encourage vigilantism. It is merely an exercise in addressing the subject of molestation, incest, and abuse, and to raise these subjects generally. The subject of sexual abuse in any form needs to be discussed and taught and talked about. How will people ever learn if no one talks about it?

What began as an effort to write a novel with my experience in therapy at its core, transformed to the point where now I hope this story will help others who are struggling through the darkness and despair of having been abused like this as a child.

It is my hope that you don't give up and that you keep looking for answers to help you heal.

REQUEST FOR REVIEW

Did this book give you any insight into your life and/or struggles, or help you in any way? I would love to hear what you think of what I have written here–your honest opinion. Honest reviews help readers find the right book for them to read. Thank you kindly.

www.ingramcontent.com/pod-product-compliance
Lightning Source LLC
LaVergne TN
LVHW040215110826
845146LV00005B/1300

9798988607601